BELLA BELLA

Jonathan London

Illustrated by

Sean London

WESTWINDS
PRESS®

Library of Congress Cataloging-in-Publication Data

Names: London, Jonathan, 1947- | London, Sean, illustrator.
Title: Bella Bella / written by Jonathan London ; illustrated by Sean London.
Description: Portland, Oregon : WestWinds Press, [2016] | Sequel to:
    Desolation Canyon. | Summary: Thirteen-year-olds Aaron and Lisa and
    their fathers, and seventeen-year-old Cassidy and his dad— embark on a
    sea kayaking trip off the coast of the Pacific Northwest that brings them
    unexpected and even terrifying adventures.
Identifiers: LCCN 2015024271 | ISBN 9780882409238 (pbk.), ISBN
    9781943328291 (e-book), ISBN 9781943328338 (hardbound)
Subjects: | CYAC: Kayaks and kayaking— Fiction. | Adventure and
    adventurers— Fiction. | Northwest, Pacific— Fiction.
Classification: LCC PZ7.L8432 Be 2016 | DDC [Fic]— dc23 LC record
    available at http://lccn.loc.gov/2015024271

Editor: Michelle McCann
Designer: Vicki Knapton

Published by WestWinds Press®
An imprint of

GRAPHIC ARTS
BOOKS®
P.O. Box 56118
Portland, Oregon 97238-6118
503-254-5591
www.graphicartsbooks.com

For Sean, Steph, Roger, Lisa, Maureen, Doug Lamb the Sailor Man, and with thanks to the people of Bella Bella.

—Jonathan London

To my mom and dad, Maureen and Jonathan, for all the bedtime stories; to my brother, Aaron, for inspiring me to be the best; and to my beautiful wife, Stephanie, for her valuable assistance, support, and love. With special thanks to Roger, Lisa, and Rowan for introducing me to the fun and adventure of island hopping in BC's wild outer central coast.

—Sean London

CONTENTS

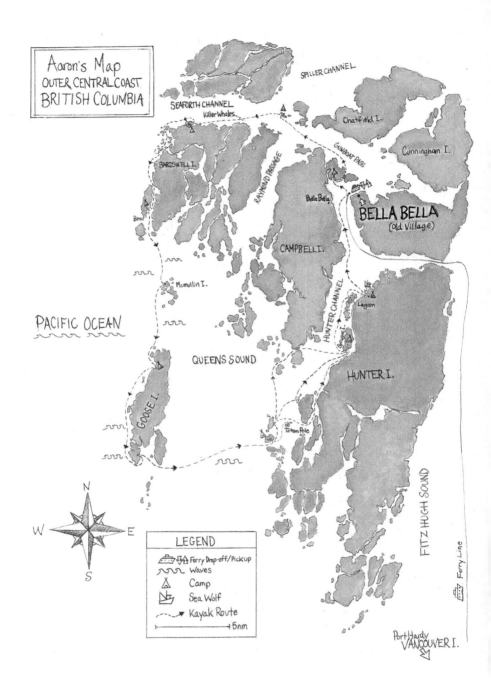

Aaron's Map
OUTER CENTRAL COAST
BRITISH COLUMBIA

SPILLER CHANNEL

SEAFORTH CHANNEL
Killer Whales

Chatfield I.

GUNBOAT PASS

Cunningham I.

BARDSWELL I.

RAYMOND PASSAGE

Bella Bella

BELLA BELLA
(Old Village)

Bear

CAMPBELL I.

McMullin I.

HUNTER CHANNEL

Lagoon

PACIFIC OCEAN

QUEENS SOUND

HUNTER I.

GOOSE I.

Totem Pole

FITZ HUGH SOUND

Ferry Line

N
W   E
S

LEGEND

Ferry Drop-off/Pickup
Waves
Camp
Sea Wolf
Kayak Route
5nm

Port Hardy
VANCOUVER I.

CHAPTER ONE

HOW HARD CAN IT BE?

We drove the windy roads over the hills to the coast and dropped a borrowed sea kayak into the shallows of Bodega Bay—the protected inner bay. The tide was out and there was no wind, and the bay was flat as glass.

Dad put on a life jacket and said, "Okay, Aaron, I'll go first. Just watch how I paddle, then you can try it."

"Geez, Dad," I said. "How hard can it be?" I stepped into the kayak and—whoosh!—it flipped over! I toppled backwards into the shallows and almost banged my head on the shore rocks.

I lay there, dazed, like a beached jellyfish.

"Aaron!" Dad said, grabbing my arm and pulling me up. "You don't just step into a kayak. You have to bend over and hold the gunnels and slide in, without tipping the boat. And you have to wear a life jacket!"

"*Geez!* I can swim, Dad!" I said. But he handed me a life jacket and I shrugged it on—unbuckled—over my sopping wet clothes. Then he helped me flip the kayak right-side up, and I tried again to climb into the kayak.

This time I squatted and placed my right foot in the center of the bottom, and held on to the sides and slipped in. No prob. Dad handed me the long, double-bladed paddle and said, "You sure about this?"

I gave him a thumbs-up and he shoved me out into the bay. Birds were watching me. A long-legged egret stood in the shallows and cocked its head. A lone loon—maybe a visitor from Canada—pointed his round red eye at me. And a family of ducks, black and white on the blue-gray water, stopped gliding and stared.

I took a deep breath and—holding the paddle almost vertical, like a canoe paddle—dug in.

ZWOOP!

Next thing I knew, I was hanging upside down in the water. It was surreal!

And it was cold.

The water was only about three feet deep so my head hit the crunchy bottom. I thought it was going to tear my scalp off. I swallowed salt water and gagged, and thought: What a way to die! Drowning—in two feet of water!

But the next moment and I was coughing and gagging and breathing air.

Air!

Dad waded in and flipped the boat right-side up. He looked horrified. But you could see he was fighting something, too.

He was fighting laughter.

I guess it was kinda funny. But it didn't bode well for my future at sea.

* * *

Let me back up a minute.

Last year, after surviving an awesome but also terrifying white-water rafting trip down the Green River through Desolation Canyon—with Roger and his daughter, Lisa, and Willie and his son, Cassidy—we'd talked about rafting or kayaking down the Owyhee or the Snake in Idaho this year.

"Change of plans, kiddo," Dad said. "We're going sea kayaking off the coast of the Pacific Northwest. Ten days of island hopping. Living off the sea."

"I thought we were going river kayaking, Dad! How come we're going sea kayaking all of a sudden?"

"Roger's idea, and I think it's a good one. He found out about a ferry that stops on Vancouver Island on its way to Queen Charlotte Island, off the west coast of British Colombia. They drop you off at midnight at an island called Bella Bella on the way up. Lisa and Cassidy have done lots of sea kayaking and they're cool with it. They wanted to do something different this year."

"Great," I said, like I didn't mean it. And I didn't.

I thought about how I'd finally mastered white-water rafting last year and was kind of an expert now: rowing through haystack waves and around boulders and keeper holes. But later in the day, I thought about Lisa. We had grown close—and I mean like more than just friends—last year in Desolation Canyon. And now I thought: ten days! With Lisa. Running on island beaches. Playing in the surf! Sweet!

A few days ago school ended. That's when Dad gave me the news that our river trip had morphed into a sea trip in kayaks, and now this morning Dad had suggested a trial run to get ready for our trip tomorrow. We were headed to Bodega Bay, on the California coast about a half hour west of where we live.

I was used to canoeing in Spring Lake and on mild stretches of the Russian River. But I'd never stepped foot in a kayak.

Dad had borrowed a one-person sea kayak from a neighbor, and I helped him strap it to the roof rack of our Toyota. I wasn't too happy about it. I'd planned to see friends today.

Do some tricks at the skate park in Sebastopol. Maybe buy a book for our long drive north.

But no. We needed a trial run. Dad had done a little sea kayaking when he was a young, and that was like a million years ago, but he figured it was like riding a bike. You never forget.

* * *

After flipping the kayak right-side up again, he pulled it in and told me to watch him. He'd show me how it's done.

So Dad climbed in and showed me how to paddle a kayak, pulling with one hand while you push with the other, dipping the double blades in smoothly, one after the other. He made it look easy—at least here on this mirror-flat water—but I acted like I wasn't watching. It was too embarrassing.

Last year I'd learned to read the river—the rapids—and how to maneuver a raft through white water. Now this was a whole new thing. In a way, it was a little like starting life all over.

In another element. *The sea.*

I could swim well, though rarely swam here in the ocean. I boogie-boarded some and was good at it. But everybody thinks the water here in California is warm.

Wrong! Down in southern California, yeah, but up here, north of San Francisco, no. It's the Humboldt Current flowing down from the Arctic, and it's cold.

How much colder would it be up north, off the Pacific Northwest coast?

Freezing. That was my guess.

That was my dread.

I thought about Lisa and Cassidy, both experienced sea kayakers. And I thought about me floundering in the ocean, like a baby pelican with a broken wing.

Now I just stood there—still dripping wet—on the rock-and-sandy shore of the smooth inner bay, and half watched Dad gliding like a swan through water.

My mouth tasted like salt.

It tasted a little like fear.

CHAPTER TWO

DOWN TO THE SEA
IN KAYAKS

I did take a spin in the kayak—with Dad calling out stuff like "Don't dig your blade in so deep!"—and after awhile I got pretty okay at it. A nervous kind of okay.

The next day, on Highway 5 driving north toward the "great Northwest" (as Dad calls it), Dad told me a little more about Bella Bella, and the whole trip. He said we'd be getting on the ferry in Port Hardy at around sunset, because that was when the ferry stopped on its way north from the city of Vancouver.

"So why don't we just get on it in Vancouver?" I asked.

"This way's quicker," Dad said. "And cheaper. Driving's fast up the coast of Vancouver Island. And I think you're gonna love Bella Bella, and all those tiny islands up there. I've never been, but I Googled photos of the area, and read a book about the native seagoing cultures up there. It will be a real adventure, kiddo."

It sounded okay, but I said, "I still don't see why we couldn't just go rafting again, or river kayaking, like you promised."

Dad shook his head. "I never promised, " he said. He made a deep sigh, and kept driving, eyes straight forward, gripping the steering wheel with both hands.

So I picked up my book, and started reading again. An awesome novel called *Peak*, about a fourteen-year-old boy— just a year older than me—who climbs Mt. Everest. It made me feel like my adventure was lesser. And yet great at the same time. As we flew by the snowy peak of Mt. Shasta, not long before crossing into Oregon, I thought of each wave crest at sea as a peak, white on top, ranging into the future.

* * *

Three long days later—and a couple hours after embarking on our boat ride from Port Hardy on the north coast of Vancouver Island—the stars above the bulkhead swayed as the ferry rolled through the deep swells, north toward Alaska.

But we weren't going to Alaska; we'd be lowered in our kayaks at midnight, off the old island village of Bella Bella, part of British Columbia, and then go island hopping.

Ashland, Crater Lake, Portland, Mt. Hood flashed by. Seattle and the Space Needle. Next we crossed the border into Canada. The glass skyscrapers of Vancouver gleamed in the sun, with awesome mountains behind them. But we didn't have time to sightsee—we had a boat to catch. We arrived in the quaint town of Horseshoe Bay just in time to make the short ferry ride to Vancouver Island.

Today, all day, we'd been driving fast up the length

of the huge island to
Port Hardy. Tall tree-covered
mountains on our left, the west, and the blue sea dotted
with tiny tree-covered islands on our right, east. Beyond the
islands was a line of impressive peaks along the west coast
of North America.

We'd embarked on the ferry at sunset, bald eagles standing in the tall trees on shore, silhouetted against the sky.

Once aboard, I was blown away by the scenery and the
sea life. Dolphins danced off the prow of the ferry as it cut
through Queen Charlotte Sound. To the east, we watched

the big jagged mountains of the mainland slide by, reddened by the low sun. Then on the left—or port side (as Roger called it)—we searched for killer whales till the sun sank like a blazing ship in the ocean.

"You look green, Aaron," Roger the Rogue said. "Keep your eyes on the horizon. That'll help settle your stomach." As I'd learned last year, he'd once been a river rat on the Rogue River, though I think most of his "roguish" days were behind him. What he did still have was a swashbuckling air, a twinkle in his eye, and a wealth of advice.

I was sitting on the hardwood deck. Roger's daughter, Lisa, stood beside me. It was totally awesome seeing her again. She was still taller than me—but barely. And she looked more drop-dead gorgeous than ever.

But right now cold salt spray hit my face. The horizon was just an invisible line where the bright stars faded into the blackness of the Pacific Ocean. Following Roger's advice, I tried to hold my gaze on it.

It didn't help.

Seasickness churned in my belly along with the butterflies of anxiety. Except for my crash course in Bodega Bay, I'd never kayaked before. And I was still a little leery about taking another trip with Cassidy. In fact, despite a cautious but growing friendship at the end of our last trip, I kind of dreaded it.

"If you're gonna spew, dude," Cassidy said, "do it downwind." He grinned.

Yeah. Good ole Cassidy. I knew he meant well, but he could be hard to take.

He was barely seventeen but seemed much older, having been to sea many times. In fact, he'd worked with his dad, Wild Man Willie, on a fishing boat off the coast of Alaska the summer before (with a new tattoo of a sea anchor on his shoulder to prove it). With a stomach like steel and a tongue like a razor, Cassidy was someone you'd never forget.

For one thing, he was unpredictable—sometimes in good ways, more often in scary ways. On our white-water rafting trip over spring break last year, he'd bombed me and Lisa with cliff-top rocks, practically drowned me in the Green River, almost caused a rattlesnake to bite Lisa, and was nasty and threatening to my dad.

But, in the end, he had saved Dad's life. In fact, I owed my father's life to him. He had proven himself a hero. And because of that, Dad and Lisa trusted him. So did I.

To a degree.

Though I was in debt to him and had a begrudging respect for him, I was still wary.

"You'll find your sea legs in no time, mate," Roger said, putting on his old-timey sea jargony voice. I rolled my eyes. He could get a little corny with his pirate act, but he was a good guy. A great guy.

"He's right," said Dad. "You'll be an 'old salt' by the end of this trip."

Old salt? "An able-bodied seaman," he said, when I gave him a puzzled look.

Roger and my dad went way back, as did Willie—to their army days in Iraq and Desert Storm. But both men couldn't be more different from Dad.

For one thing, like me—though we lived near the sea—Dad was a landlubber next to them and Cassidy. And even Lisa.

Lisa had gone sea kayaking many times. And at thirteen, she was probably the prettiest tomboy to ever sail the seven seas.

I tried to stand up, held on to the rail for a second, and slowly lowered myself back down on the deck. Lisa squatted behind me and gripped me around my chest. Her touch sent a thrill through my body.

"Upsy-daisy," she said. With her help I stood up, lurched with the roll of the ship, and grasped the deck rail.

"Listen up, you scallywags!" bawled Willie, borrowing a word from Roger's pirate lingo. A powerfully built man, Willie could belt out orders that made your hair stand at attention. "We've got forty-five minutes to get belowdecks, gather our gear, and rig up our kayaks for off-loading," he called out as he took off his floppy Aussie-style hat and gave my backside a whack.

"You okay, kiddo?" Dad asked. He had bony hands and a body like a broken crate—all bones and awkward angles. Sometimes he was a talker, but these were the first three words he'd spoken to me all evening.

"I'm good," I lied.

I said, "Later," to Lisa, then I led the way, swaying and staggering, belowdecks to our pile of gear, which would be our "tools of survival" for the next ten days.

Those were Dad's words.

As on our river trip through Desolation Canyon, most of our gear was stuffed into watertight rubber dry bags. I slipped my arm through the strap of one and hoisted it onto my back. I sighed, realizing we'd each have to make two or three trips lugging our loads to the staging area on the second deck.

Roger had sold us his old sea kayak on our way north (we met up in Grants Pass, Oregon). Now three long, sleek, double sea kayaks were stacked on deck like stiff, polished crocodiles in the glow of the yellow storm light. Four grizzled deckhands peered at our growing pile of stuff with growing alarm.

Having been up since 3:00 AM, we were well beyond tired. Now it was almost midnight, and the sound of the sea slapping the hull reverberated in my bones as if I were in a submarine awaiting a depth charge from above.

Since it was impossible in Bella Bella to off-load kayaks from the ferry directly to the wharf—no real harbor there, not for seagoing ferries, anyway—our kayaks had to be lowered into the sea by lines and a winch.

With us in them! A drop of about twenty-five feet, maybe more.

"Buckle your seat belts," Cassidy said to me and Dad, as he and his dad, Willie, squeezed into their fully loaded eighteen-foot kayak.

The deckhands slipped two slings beneath it—one fore and one aft of their cockpits. The winch engine revved, the boom creaked, and Willie and Cassidy were lifted over the deck rail and slowly lowered into the sea.

In the starlight, the kayak and its occupants were just silhouettes.

Sick silhouettes! Scary and almost majestic.

Soon they were followed by Lisa and her dad.

Now it was our turn. As I climbed into the forward cockpit, I started to sweat in the cold sea air. I looked down. Big mistake. The water was choppy and the ferry was swaying and our kayak was swinging.

Once again, the winch engine revved, the boom creaked, and up we went. The deckhands carefully swung us outboard, slowly, and we swung there, dangling, holding our breath, clenching the sides of our cockpits.

And it looked like a very long ways down. I tightened my life jacket. I squeezed my eyes shut. Then I opened them again. They felt like they were bulging in their sockets.

I felt like throwing up. I took a deep breath and held it again. My fingernails dug into the sides of our kayak as we were slowly lowered toward the cauldron below.

Suddenly, the line attached to the forward sling snapped with a loud *PING!*

We started to plummet. My stomach flew into my mouth. I heard the scream of a gull—but it was coming from me.

CHAPTER THREE

FIRST NATIONS

We're gonna sink! We're gonna lose all our gear! Geez, I thought, we're gonna drown!

Our kayak dropped and slid at an angle into the dark water below. *SPLOOSH!* The front of the kayak plowed in and most of the boat went underwater. Good thing we were zipped into our cockpits so no water could get into the boat. Then our kayak popped back up and slammed the surface with a huge splash.

Our companions watched with mouths wide open until Cassidy let out a hoot and a laugh.

Soon—though still shaken—we were all laughing, shouting "Thanks!" and "Anchors away!" to the deckhands, with more sarcasm than gratitude.

But dread soon started to seep back in—at least for me. Now here we were, three kayaks at midnight, rising and falling with the low swells off the village of Bella Bella, the sea a scattered nest of stars, and we—lost birds.

As we drifted there, not sure which way to go, Roger

went back to telling us about Bella Bella, "All this land around us is an Indian reservation—"

"It's called a 'reserve' in Canada, Dad," Lisa cut in. "And native people are called 'First Nations' or aboriginals." We were soon to learn that she'd been reading a book about the area, just like my dad.

"Thanks, sweetheart," said Roger. "Anyway, it's the home of the Heiltsuk or the Bella Bella, one of the many First

Nations of the Pacific Northwest Coast. And—unfortunately for us—it's off-limits at night to kayakers and campers without permission."

At this hour, Bella Bella was just a scattering of lights, like a few fallen stars amid the vast darkness.

We drifted a few more moments in silence. Then Roger said, "We'll have to find some place to put in for the night. Okay? So let's roll, mates!" This in his usual jolly voice—despite the late hour.

"Uh, which way, Rog?" my dad asked tentatively. He sounded as lost as I felt.

"North. We'll be heading north, and then west in the morning."

"Actually," Cassidy said, "you don't have a clue where we're gonna put in tonight, do ya? I say we sneak into Bella Bella—"

"Cassidy—" Willie said.

"It's okay, Willie," said Roger. "He's right about not knowing where to go. We're just winging it. We'll just have to find an island by blind luck, or paddle all night trying."

"I'm getting cold, Dad," Lisa said. "Can we get going now?" She wasn't one to complain, but there was a chilling sea breeze beneath the summer stars, and Dad and I were a little wet from our plunge, and getting colder by the minute. I was still seasick, and ready to dive under a warm rock in any dry place, and sleep.

"Let's get this show on the road!" Willie barked.

"*Yee-haw!*" sang Cassidy.

"And *yippie-ki-yay!*" Roger yodeled, then took off with Lisa, heading north. Cassidy and Willie paddled after them, with Dad and me following behind.

At first, Dad and I kept whacking our paddles together. I was up front, so I figured Dad had to synchronize with me. After awhile, we got better at it.

And it was kinda cool. Our kayak rode so low, it felt like we were inside the water. Gliding through the water like a pro.

Given that this was our maiden voyage in a sea kayak, I think we were pretty awesome.

After awhile, we started to cluster close together and slow down. We were getting tired. Willie started telling us stories, maybe to keep us alert. "When Cass and I worked in Alaska, we heard stories about fishing boats smuggling drugs . . . or illegal immigrants. Back in 1999—maybe you heard about this—the Canadian police intercepted boats and ships with hundreds of illegal immigrants from China in their holds, being smuggled in by human traffickers—"

"I don't think they say 'illegal immigrants' anymore," Lisa cut in. "They say 'undocumented migrants,' or 'undocumented immigrants' now."

Willie laughed. "I can't keep up with the politically correct lingo, Lisa, but thanks. Anyway, I've heard that a lot of, uh, undocumented migrants are flying in from China now with false passports, but there's still some coming in on fishing bo—"

Suddenly we heard the sound of a motor zooming our way. A searchlight swept the water and a motorboat filled with shadowy human shapes spun around us, rocking our kayaks in its wake.

The driver slowed the motor to an idle and said, "Hey. It's after midnight, folks. What are you doing out here? Fishin' without a license?"

"Uhh, umm," Roger stammered.

Then, after what felt like an eternity, we heard some laughter from their boat.

"Aw, I'm just messin' with ya," the driver said, chuckling. He shifted the searchlight away from our eyes, adjusted his baseball cap, and said, "You get dropped off by the ferry? We don't get many kayakers here. Anyway, we call Bella Bella 'the Rock,' and you can't camp there. But no worries, I'll hook you up with a place to camp. Follow me."

I think we all let out a sigh of relief, then paddled after him as he slowly took off.

"Crazy Indians," Cassidy said, but just loud enough for us to hear.

"Zip it!" said Willie.

"That's so not cool!" Lisa said.

"Sorry," Cassidy said. "Crazy First Nations."

"Shut up!" Lisa cried. She liked Cassidy—a lot, I feared—but he could get under her skin. He could get under anybody's skin. I don't even think he was trying to be mean, just get noticed or something. He liked attention.

I reminded myself that Cassidy had no mother and lived a rough life on the edge with Willie. And I happened to know that his best friend was a Spokane Indian. But does that make it okay? I wondered.

We paddled hard along the shore, following the motor-boat, till we finally came to a small cove. Tall, dark trees loomed over us. And there, around twenty yards from shore, floated a large wooden barnacle–encrusted raft.

"Here you go!" said the driver. "You can sleep on the raft. And you're in luck—no rain tonight. We get loads of rain up in these parts."

"Much appreciated, pard," Willie said, and we all thanked him. Willie came from Eastern Washington, out in dry ranch country, and he said "pard" in a kindly, country way. Except when he was mad. And right now, he wasn't.

"No problem," said the driver. "Just watch out you don't roll off the raft and fall into the drink!" A few hoots and howls from the motorboat as he gunned it into the dark and disappeared.

We slid in alongside the anchored raft and I climbed out—careful not to tip the boat—and tied us off before Dad could get up and out with his gangly legs.

The raft was just large enough for all six of us to unroll our sleeping bags.

There was no moon that I could see, but the sky was

swarming with stars, and our eyes had grown accustomed to the star-pricked dark. We had eaten dinner aboard the ferry, so we didn't have to set up a camp stove and cook before bedding down. I managed to lay out my down bag between my dad and Lisa, and munched on an energy bar.

Lisa said, "Wow! That sky is crazy, Aaron! Just look at those stars!"

"I know, right? Amazing!" It was like it was just the two of us, and this was our own personal sky.

Dad wanted to point out the constellations but I cut him off. "I gotta sleep now, Dad. It's the middle of the night!"

"Fine, kiddo. Sleep tight."

I swallowed the last of my energy bar and rolled over toward Lisa, but now I realized I couldn't talk to her after telling Dad I had to go to sleep

But I whispered, "'Night, Miss Starlight."

She poked me—hard—with her sharp elbow and went, "*Ewww!* A little cheesy, dontcha think, Aaron?" Then she giggled, and rolled away.

That night, cocooned in our sleeping bags, we floated peacefully under the stars. The raft gently rocked and lulled us off to sleep.

CHAPTER FOUR

WOLF!

In the morning I awoke to Cassidy and Lisa whispering. I couldn't hear what they were saying, but I didn't like it. Their heads were close together and that really bothered me. I was going to say, "Good morning" or something stupid like that, but then Cassidy started tickling her, which made the raft rock.

Lisa swore and promised death to her tormentor. She hated to be tickled.

"Let me go, you freak!" she half-squealed and half-giggled.

"I thought you liked to be tickled! It's fun. Laugh! Laugh! Laugh!"

"Cassidy!" Willie barked.

Cassidy stopped tickling her and the raft stopped rocking. "Chill, Willie! I'm just foolin' with her." He always called his dad "Willie." I never once heard him say "Dad."

Lisa sat up and slugged him on the arm, hard. But you could see a glint of amusement in her eyes—a glint that cut me to the quick.

"Kids," Willie said with a sigh and flopped back onto his sleeping mat. Dad and Roger groaned and rolled over in their bags, and went back to sleep.

I looked around. The sun was aglow, making a halo above the trees north of Bella Bella. A bald eagle glared down at us from a shoreline spruce.

I wondered why it was called Bella Bella. I knew it meant beautiful in Spanish and Italian, but why say it twice? It sounded like an Italian guy adoring a beautiful girl, or a dish of pasta. Bella Bella!

* * *

Half an hour later the sun burst through the trees, warmed the morning mist away, and nudged Dad and Roger awake.

"Java," Roger mumbled. He rose to his elbows and sniffed the air for coffee. He'd slept with his trademark red bandana on his pony-tailed head and, with his wicked reddish gray goatee, he looked like a sleepy, benign pirate.

Willie had already made a strong pot of coffee on his small Svea stove. Soon we all sipped the hot black brew on our first morning at sea.

* * *

An hour later we were far out in the Inland Passage—off Gunboat Pass—quietly paddling north through the island-dotted water world.

Gunboat Pass. That name put a thrill of wonder into me.

There must be some reason it was called that. Maybe it dated back to pirate days. Or maybe boats smuggling drugs or refugees.

But we didn't see any gunboats—at least, I didn't think we saw any. We saw a couple of ships and barges, all far away.

Ice water dripped down my arms—ice water flowing down from the Arctic—but the spray skirt attached to the rim of the cockpit and cinched around my waist kept me dry below.

My back and shoulders ached, but after awhile I got into the rhythm and almost forgot about the pain. I've come a long way since Bodega Bay, I thought. In more ways than one.

Hey! That rhymes! I always had a pen in my pocket and I thought of writing it down, but it was too much trouble with my spray skirt on. So I sang softly to myself: *I've come a long way/from Bodega Bay*, as we sliced through the surface with our double-bladed paddles. We glided quickly enough to create a breeze, but quietly enough not to startle the nearby sea lions, who poked their heads out of the water and watched us with their huge dark eyes.

We'd be island-hopping along this hidden coast for the next nine and a half days, living largely off what we caught and gathered from the sea. We'd be going counterclockwise in a big, jagged circle: first north and west through Seaforth Channel, then south through the open Pacific, then east and back north to Bella Bella. Roger and Willie had pored over charts for weeks as they planned this trip. But weather was an unknown . . . and to me, it was all an unknown.

* * *

In late afternoon we grounded ashore in an island cove. The tide was out, and we had to haul our kayaks high above the tide line, slipping and sliding over small round stones. The shoreline here was rocky and wild. We tethered our boats to tree snags for the night and set out to scout the island.

We followed a deer path through dense spruce and cedar—Roger naming the trees—and on across a narrow spit of land, coming out on a long, white, sandy beach facing the ocean. Lisa kicked off her shoes and twirled around barefoot in the sand, her black ponytail spinning. Breakers crashed and boomed, sending up a fine spray.

"This looks like a good place to camp tonight," I said

"Could get windy," Roger warned.

"Keeps the bugs away," Willie said.

"Roger that," said Dad, making a rare joke. Or is it a pun?

I pulled off my river sandals and ran off down the beach—with Lisa at my heels. She moved like the wind with her long, slim legs, but this year I could match her stride for stride. Last year she was two inches taller than me; now I was getting tall and gangly.

Breathless, we stopped running, our feet sinking in wet sand. It was intense having Lisa at my side. I picked up a flat round stone and skimmed it across the backwash, where

it smacked a breaker and flapped up like a startled bird. Lisa rummaged for a stone, wound up, and skimmed it like a pro. It bounced six times at least.

"Good one," I said, winging another stone. "It's awesome here. But I miss the river rafting a bit. Wasn't that crazy fun last year in Desolation Canyon?"

"Yeah, and crazy scary, too," said Lisa. "I could do without all that drama." Meaning the trouble we'd had with Cassidy, and my dad's accident. She flicked suds at me from her fingers. I danced away, and that's when I saw the deep tracks in the wet sand.

"Wolf tracks, I think."

"Or a very large dog's," Lisa said.

The tracks ran inland toward the dry sand, where they faded out. "Hey! Guys! Wolf tracks!" I yelled.

"What?" Roger yelled.

"*Wolf!*"

Cassidy came running, followed by the others, and squatted down. Willie stooped beside him and pushed back his big floppy hat. "Lone wolf, all right. He might be back there in the trees right now, watching us. These tracks are fresh."

"I didn't know there were wolves here," I said.

"Wolves, bears, deer, raccoons. They swim out from the mainland," said Roger.

"Cool," I said.

"Sweet," said Lisa. She was afraid of nothing. Me, I wasn't

so sure, really, about being on a small island with large bears and wolves.

I heard the sound of a motor and looked offshore. What looked like a commercial fishing boat was puttering by. A man stood on deck staring at us. I waved, but he didn't wave back.

We were on a deserted island, miles from anyone else. The man was big, grim faced, brutal looking, with his hair tied in a bushy graying ponytail. His yellow-tinted sunglasses blazed in the sun.

Like the eyes of a wolf.

CHAPTER FIVE

DINNER FOR A *SEA WOLF*

That's strange, I thought, following the big fishing boat with my eyes. Fishermen usually wave back when you wave—at least on the fishing boats in Bodega Bay they do. I think it's some kind of etiquette of the sea, or something like that.

Even with sunglasses on, it felt like he had looked right through me. I turned to Lisa, who was standing nearby. She was staring at the boat, or its captain. And she was hugging herself, as if she were cold.

Maybe he gave her the creeps, too.

* * *

Later, Roger and Willie went out fishing in the cove. Dad and I lugged our gear across the spit and found a good spot to pitch our tent. It gave us a view of the open sea to the west, yet offered us a bit of shelter back in the brush.

I joined Lisa and Cassidy on the beach. Cassidy was doing standing backflips, one after the other, like an acrobat. He was stripped to his bathing trunks, and his tattooed muscles rippled in the sun. Lisa acted unimpressed, watching only out of the corners of her eyes. She was lounging in a blue bikini, twirling her dark hair with a finger.

When Cassidy saw me coming, he dashed toward me to tackle me. I faked left and juked him. But he kept running, swooped Lisa off the sand, and threw her, shrieking, over his shoulder. Then he sprinted down the surf line with her hair hanging down and her body bouncing.

I skimmed stones and tried to act as if it didn't bother me, but it did. Something unspoken caught like a stone in my throat. Geez, I can't believe this was happening to me again. I thought I'd grown out of this since last year. Jealousy was an ax to my ego, and it cut me in half. Lisa was the one and only girl I've ever felt this way about, and I didn't know what to do about it.

The hurt receded for a while as we all sat around eating the salmon Roger and Willie had caught. Like last year on the Green River, Wild Man Willie was the camp cook. But because of our kayaks, we had to travel light here, so he had no Dutch oven and multi-burner stand-up camp stove to work his wonders. What he did have was fresh-caught fish and a driftwood fire to cook it over. As Willie said, "Outta the sea and into the pan!"

"Yes!" Roger said. "Nothin' seasons fish like sea salt and hard fun!"

"Everything tastes good in the outback of nowhere," Dad said.

"This isn't nowhere, man," Roger said. "This is the middle of paradise!"

Lisa leaned against a huge weathered drift log beside me and let her bare shoulder, still warm from the sun, brush against mine. I swear, my heart glowed.

Dusk comes late in the northern summer, and the fire had died to coals by the time the sun simmered in the sea. Lisa wiggled her toes in the still warm sand and turned to me.

"Let's go skinny-dipping, Aaron!" she said, her eyes shining like wet agates.

My heart did cartwheels and my mouth dropped open.

"Just kidding!" she said, and jabbed me with a sharp elbow.

* * *

That night I dreamed I was giving Lisa a piggyback ride through the surf. It was so real that I was sure it was happening, and yet I couldn't believe it was happening. It was too good to be true.

But later I had a whole other kind of dream.

The bad kind. A nightmare.

I was alone in our kayak, lost in the fog, when a large fishing boat, shrouded in mist, came into sight. It was coming around the tip of an island. I glanced around, looking for my dad, for Roger and Lisa and the rest, but they were nowhere in sight. Then the boat was about a hundred yards away and slowly turning toward me. And standing in the bow was the man in the yellow sunglasses.

He was looking down the barrel of a rifle, aiming right between my eyes.

I woke to the sound of a wolf howling somewhere in the distance. My skin crawled like it was swarming with baby jellyfish.

* * *

In the morning, the dreams were still with me. Conflicting dreams. One good, the other bad.

But I had no time to unravel the two dreams from each other. It was time to get up, gather driftwood for the fire, eat breakfast, scrub plates and cups, roll up the sleeping bags, take down the tent. In other words, break camp and load the kayaks. Our daily ritual.

It was weird, seeing Lisa in the morning. Almost bumping into her while shoveling beans onto our plate. It's always weird seeing someone you just dreamt about. Embarrassing, somehow.

And while I ate, I kept looking out toward the point, listening for the sound of a fishing boat (which, in my nightmare, had become a gunboat, of sorts).

Rags of mist hung in the trees around the cove as we pushed off with the ebbing tide. Bald eagles adorned the high branches like Christmas ornaments, and ravens flapped and cackled over a dead beached salmon. Just as the

sun broke through the fog, an eagle swooped down and snatched the prize, scattering the ravens like tattered black umbrellas in a storm.

The day was long and hard, but never boring. We paddled by a family of sea otters—who followed us for an hour—and watched for whales and dolphins. I kept an eye out for the fishing boat from yesterday—the one in my dream—and thought about smugglers.

Suddenly Roger shouted, "Orcas!"

At first I couldn't see them. We drifted close together and shaded our eyes.

"They're deep diving," Roger said. "They'll be back up in a few minutes."

"Killer whales!" I said, feeling fear and awe at the same time.

"Some call 'em sea wolves," Willie said, "because they attack like a pack of wolves, surrounding schools of salmon or separating out sea lions and even whales, and workin' together. A pack can attack and skin a blue whale alive."

I was fascinated but creeped out at the same time.

"One time on the coast of Alaska," Willie said, "I saw killer whales flinging sea lions like mice. They turned the water bloodred."

"Sick!" said Cassidy.

"Ugh," said Lisa.

"Yeah," said Roger. "They can slither right up onto a beach, snatch a sea lion or harbor seal, and wiggle back into the surf."

"Do they ever attack kayakers?" I asked, trying not to sound nervous.

"I've never heard of one attacking a kayaker," said Roger

"Well, kayakers have gone missing," Willie said, dipping his big flappy hat into the cold water and flopping it back on his head. "Nobody knows if they were attacked by orcas or not."

Just then the pod of orcas surfaced, breached, and breathed in unison—great spouts bursting in the sun. They were maybe a hundred yards away, rolling straight toward us, their tall, sharp dorsal fins cutting through the waves.

Will they capsize us? I wondered. Would they eat us like harbor seals?

The orcas were maybe fifty yards away now. Forty. Thirty. Twenty yards. *Ten!*

The whales swam right between our kayaks, their dorsal fins slicing the surface! Shiny black-and-white monsters of the sea, beautiful and terrifying, speeding smoothly and unstoppable right through us. Their huge wakes rocked us, almost capsizing our kayaks.

Suddenly something bumped our kayak and I let out a yell. I was sure this was the end: *Dinner for a sea wolf.*

Our boat slammed down, and there between our kayaks rose a column of bubbles, followed by something huge and dark.

Getting closer and closer.

CHAPTER SIX

GUNSHOTS AT DAWN

*B**LOUACH!*

It wasn't an orca, after all. It was a huge sea lion, rolling big, panicky black eyes at us. It had been chased by the orcas, and maybe circled back. It went BLOUACH again, slapped its tail, and plunged back down, the water boiling up between us.

We held our breath and braced for the orcas to come back. But they didn't come. I figured they were still stalking the sea lion, or something else just as big and juicy.

Later we saw their spouts off to the south, like plumes of mist.

"Wow!" Willie said. "That was a Steller's sea lion. I bet it weighed 1,500 pounds! And they're rarely at sea this time of year!"

"Okay, biology class is over," Cassidy said. "When do we hit the beach?"

* * *

We beached an hour later on the sheltered leeward side of a small, rocky island. It was dense with dark spruce and Sitka cedar scented the air.

We hauled our kayaks far up the sand, above the tide line piled with seaweed. Lisa and I wanted to go exploring, but, as ever, we had chores to do.

Set up camp. Gather firewood. We worked quickly so we'd have time to run off on our own.

On the windward side of the island, Lisa and I explored the most beautiful tide pools I'd ever seen. Colorful starfish stuck to the rocks as if glued there, and sea anemones waved exotic flowery tendrils—sticky to the touch, as they closed on our fingers.

Sure enough, we weren't alone for long. Cassidy came hunkering through the scrub, right out to our tide pool. Followed by Roger, Willie, and Dad.

"Really?" I said. They just couldn't get that maybe we'd like to be alone sometimes. Just hanging out. Having fun.

Cassidy sloshed in and pried a large mussel from a boulder. Then he pulled what Dad called the "bivalve" shells apart to expose the glistening meat. He bared his teeth as if he were about to eat it raw.

"Yum!" said Lisa. "But you're supposed to steam or boil them till they open, dumbwit!"

"Stop fooling around, Cassidy," Willie said. "Mussels are on the menu tonight!"

I jumped up on a rock and flexed my bicep. "I got muscles!" I punned.

Nobody laughed. I think at least two people groaned.

Including Lisa, rolling her eyes.

Willie came scampering back with a bucket, and we all chipped in, prying mussels from the wet rocks for dinner.

* * *

That evening we ate another great Wild Man Willie special: fresh mussels steamed with garlic and scallions and lemon juice, all poured over linguini, and sea salted and peppered to taste.

"What, no raw mussels for you, Cassidy?" asked Lisa.

"Are you kidding me?" he said. "I'd rather eat snot!"

"Gross!" Lisa said, but she laughed. And I almost did, too.

As our cook fire sizzled and snapped, we watched the sinking sun set a fleet of thin clouds afire, like blazing ships in a sea of blue.

"Willie?" I said. "You said kayakers have gone missing, but nobody knows why. You think it's got anything to do with . . . you know . . . smugglers?"

"Smugglers, maybe. Or killer whales. Or freak waves. Who knows? But smugglers . . . they don't want nothin' to do with us if we have nothin' to do with them," Willie said, dead serious.

"You're trippin', Aaron," Cassidy said. "You got smugglers on your mind! What you need to watch out for is GIANT OCTOPUSES!" Suddenly Cassidy threw a heavy arm around my neck, locked me in a chokehold, and rubbed my skull with his knuckles.

He pulled his grip tighter. Air shut off to my lungs, and my eyes watered. I grabbed his wrist and yanked. He finally let go, and I gasped for breath.

"What's gotten into you?" Willie snapped. His eyes burned like embers in the dusk.

"It's cool," I said, but it wasn't. I was shaking and my Adam's apple felt like it was crushed. I wanted to strike back at Cassidy, but it really wasn't in my nature. I just simmered in silence, trying to recall the other Cassidy. The hero beneath the mask. But it was hard.

"Sometimes you're so immature, Cassidy," Lisa said. "Seriously." He just stared at her. As usual, you couldn't read what was going on behind those steely eyes, and it was scary.

"Okay, so, who wants to hear a joke?" said Roger. Not waiting for an answer, he said, "A termite goes into a bar and says, 'Is the bar tender here?'"

Everybody laughed, except me. "I don't get it," I said.

And then I did. "Oh, the termite asks if the bar is tender here, because termites eat wood! And the wood is tend—"

Cassidy pushed me over into the sand. Then he yanked me back up and brushed the sand off me and said, "I got a better one. An orca goes into a bar and asks, 'Is the bartender here?' Then it eats him. CHOMP!" Now Cassidy made like he was going bite my head off.

Willie jumped up and reminded us we had dishes to wash before it got too dark. (Since he did the cooking, he didn't have to wash dishes. That was the idea, anyway.)

"That's whack, Willie! Wash your own dishes and I'll wash mine," Cassidy said, flinging sand.

Willie glared; it looked like his face would burst.

"I can wash the dishes, no sweat," Dad said. I couldn't believe it. Last year Dad and Cassidy were always in each other's faces, at each other's throats. I remembered the time Cassidy even knocked him down. Now here was Dad, standing up for him. It was bewildering. And it made me angry.

Cassidy grinned. "I'm good, man. No worries."

We gathered the dirty silverware and plates—Cassidy too—and scrubbed them in a patch of sand near the water. Nobody said anything. I was still steaming. I knew he was just a jokester, but it gets old. It gets old.

Finally I said, "'Night," and started back to our tent. I wanted to be with Lisa, but not with Cassidy around. It burned me up; I literally felt hot, though it was a cool evening.

I brushed my teeth and wiped sand off my feet, and by the time I crawled into our tent, the crescent moon had set and the sky was packed with stars, so close it felt like you could fling out a net and catch them like fish.

Dad was still up chewing the fat with Roger and Willie by the dying fire. I wondered, with a pang, what Lisa and Cassidy were doing. They were always giving each other a hard time, but I guessed it was just a kind of flirting, really. I wished I had an easier time with girls. With Lisa, anyway. Last year, by the end of our trip, we were getting along real great. It was cool between us. We could just hang out and be ourselves. We trusted each other.

We liked each other.

I closed my eyes, and Lisa's image burned a hole in my mind.

* * *

BOOM! BOOM! BOOM!

I woke at dawn to the sound of gunshots thundering

and echoing between the islands, cracking the morning wide open.

Dad and I sat bolt upright in our sleeping bags. The thumping of my heart in my ears almost drowned it out.

But not quite.

CHAPTER SEVEN

GOOEY DUCK DIVERS

The sound of gunshots gradually faded into silence. The sound of the waves. There was no way to know if the gunshots came from our island, a boat, or a nearby island. Whatever, they came from somewhere pretty close.

Dad and I looked at each other. His eyes were puffy from sleep, and his hollow cheeks were shadowed by three days' growth. We both crawled toward the tent flap at the same time and poked our heads out into the rosy dawn.

Roger and Willie were already outside, squatting around the fire ring from last night, rubbing their hands. We quickly dressed and wobbled out to join them.

"Poachers, I bet," Willie said, snapping a thick stick with his bare hands and preparing to build a fire. "There's Sitka black-tailed deer out here on these islands, and no Fish and Game folks prowling around. No law at all."

"Could be crazies," Roger said. "Firing off at seabirds or eagles, just for fun." He fired a match, held it to a twist of dry moss, and blew softly on it before pushing it beneath a small tepee of kindling.

"Or commercial fishermen," Willie said. "They'll shoot seals and sea lions—even otters—'cause they compete with them for the fish and crab and abalone."

I thought of the boat captain with the yellow sunglasses and gray ponytail.

"Heck," Roger said, "it could be anybody. Neptune's grandmother!"

"Whoever it is," Dad said, "I think we should move out now. Put some space between us and them." He nervously scratched his bearded chin.

Cassidy came crawling out of his tent like a sleepy bear and said, "Whoa! Dreamt I heard gunshots. BAM!" and he fired an imaginary rifle, right between my eyes.

* * *

An hour later we were nosing into the crisp current of the straights with a strong wind out of the east at our backs. The gale lulled for a while after our break for lunch, and we floated, silent as feathers, by a small raft of sea otters wrapped in kelp, catching their afternoon nap.

Peace came over us amid the pristine islands. And I'd almost forgotten about the gunshots when we glided around a point, and there, in the center of a small group of islands— like a meadow surrounded by forest—floated the fishing boat we'd seen a couple of days before. Its anchor was dropped, and the man with the yellow sunglasses was standing in the bow, watching our approach. The sun glinted off his reflective sunglasses, and again I was reminded of the eyes of a wolf.

And of his nighttime visitations to my dreams.

My stomach contracted. Call it a gut response.

"Hello the boat!" Roger called, drifting up toward its bow.

The man just stood there staring. A rifle leaned against the cabin behind him. That might account for the gunshots, I thought. Then I noticed for the first time the name on the hull: *Sea Wolf.*

Fits, I thought to myself. This was seriously giving me the creeps.

We clustered near the bow, shipped our paddles, and gazed back up at him in a tense silence.

Finally Willie spoke. "Out here fishin, pard?" he said. The brow of his hat threw his face into shadow.

"Nope." The man bit the word off, like a mobster snipping the end off a Havana cigar. "Geoduck diving." (I thought for a long time it was spelled "gooey duck," because that's how it sounds.)

"Any luck?"

"We'll see, won't we?" the man said. He turned his gaze away and trained it down into the dark water off his prow, where a column of bubbles was rising to the surface.

Suddenly the water boiled up before us, and the masked head of a scuba diver popped up. He looked at us and lifted up the biggest clam I'd ever seen. It must have weighed nine or ten pounds.

"Wong!" growled the man on the bow. "Get up here!"

Wong lowered the giant clam, then pulled up his mask. "Hi! You like geoduck?" he said with a strong Chinese accent. "I get them for my brother in Chinatown. Vancouver. He has a very good restaurant. You want, I'll give you one. Good to eat!"

"Wong!" snapped the man on the bow.

A bruised silence filled the air around us.

"Thanks," Willie said to the diver, "but we gotta be going now. Got to make camp before the tide changes." The diver nodded, then swam to the fishing boat and started climbing up a ladder on the side.

We were paddling away when we heard a loud thump against the hull of the *Sea Wolf* and a muffled, heartrending cry from within.

* * *

"What was that all about?" I asked when we met up later in a huddle of kayaks, while Roger and Willie consulted their sea charts. A gull screamed and swooped overhead.

"Which?" Willie said, not lifting his eyes from the plastic-sheathed chart. "The geoduck diver or that cry from their boat?"

"Both."

"I never even heard of geoducks," Lisa said.

"The Chinese consider them delicacies," said Willie, still not looking up from his sea chart. "They're chopped up for a seafood chowder. Chinese restaurants pay a small fortune for 'em. A geoduck diver can earn four hundred a day harvesting them."

"Awesome!" said Cassidy. "Why don't we do that? We'd get rich!"

"Can it!" Willie said.

"So why was the captain so mean?" I said. "He should've been happy if he's making good money."

"For one thing," Willie said, "I doubt he had a license. Big fine if you're caught without one. And I don't even think it's legally the season for harvesting them."

"Do you think they're hiding something?" I asked. "Do you think it's maybe a front?"

"A front?" Lisa said. "For what?" A big fist of wind blindsided our kayaks, and one of the sea charts almost sailed away. Willie wrestled it back down.

"Maybe they're really smuggling . . . immigrants or something," I said.

"It's not time to be worrying about smugglers," Willie cut in.

"But there's something going on in that boat, right?" I said.

Willie didn't say any more, but I could see he was thinking. And his silence was like a slowly burning fuse.

I couldn't get the sound of that heartrending cry inside the boat out of my head. Humans? Traffickers? Smugglers?

Seriously scary stuff.

Thinking this, I saw in my mind's eye, the man with the sunglasses.

And he was looking at me.

PIRATES

About an hour later we pulled up on a tiny island with a sandy beach to take a break. Lisa and I sat down and let baby wavelets lap our feet. At one point she pushed me and I almost toppled over, so I pushed her back.

But then we stopped and fell silent.

I expected Cassidy to come over, but he was sitting with Willie and Roger and my dad on the other side of a boulder, maybe twenty feet away, hiding us from their view. They were talking with low voices, but a soft breeze seemed to be blowing the words our way.

Lisa hopped up and started walking slowly down the beach, stooping to pick up shells and stuff. I was about to jump up and follow her when the breeze brought Willie's words right to me.

"Yeah, could be stowaways in that boat," he said.

"That's messed up," answered another voice. Willie was talking to Cassidy.

"Now don't go telling Lisa and Aaron. No need to scare

them when we don't know what we're dealing with."

Geez! I thought. They're treating us like kids, but they're fine telling Cassidy?

"Illegal immigrants from China," Willie said, "shell out lots of moola to get away and join their relatives in Vancouver. The average worker in China makes something like four thousand bucks a year. That's peanuts next to what they can make here. So they pay Chinese 'snakeheads' to sneak them in. And sometimes they get swindled. Lots of criminals, human traffickers, get into the action. Big bucks, man. Big bucks."

"So you think that's what we heard in that boat— stowaways?"

"Could be," Willie said. "I doubt it. But could be."

"Don't you think we should stay away from them?" said another voice. My dad's voice. "And then report them to the Coast Guard or whoever?"

So now my dad is talking about all this stuff without me!

I leaned forward, my stomach contracting into tight knots.

"We're jumping to conclusions here," Roger said. "We don't know anything. People fish or dive for goeducks off-season all the time. They just try not to get caught."

Dad turned to Cassidy. "What do you think, Cassidy?"

"I think that we don't run from them. We should jump their ship and see what they've got in there."

"That's the worst idea I've heard all day!" Willie said.

I couldn't take it anymore. I got up and walked over to where they were talking, and they abruptly tried to change the subject.

"Why don't you want to know what *I* think, huh, Dad?" I said between clenched teeth. "Why are you asking Cassidy? Don't you trust my judgment?"

"Aaron! We didn't know you were there. I—" my dad stammered.

"Well here I am."

"Okay, so . . ." Dad scratched his graying stubble and looked everywhere but at my face. "So . . . what do you think?"

I was so angry I couldn't speak. My face felt clenched like a fist.

Willie interrupted before I could think of an answer. "I say we move out now. We're wasting time." He climbed to his feet and started pushing his kayak into the surf.

* * *

When we were all back out in our kayaks, I thought about what I'd heard. They might be smugglers after all! I'd been thinking it all along. Cassidy said I was imagining things, but I wasn't. I was listening to my instincts. Willie and Roger said not to worry about it, but that made me worry even more. And it made me madder the more I thought about it. Dad and the others didn't think I was worth asking. They didn't value my opinion—even though I'd been right. What was *that* all about?

We paddled hard for about an hour, then huddled up for a short rest, drifting on the slow swells like a raft of sea lions taking a snooze. Nobody said anything.

"So then, they're like modern-day pirates, sort of?" I said, breaking the silence. I suddenly felt foolish. A white-cap slapped our hull and broke over it, splashing me. The wind was picking up.

"Pirates?" Cassidy began to sing, "'Fifteen men on a dead man's chest—'"

"'Yo-ho-ho and a barrel o' rum!'" Roger joined in, trying to break the tension, and they both cracked up.

"Dad! Really?" Lisa snapped at him. "Pirates? What about pirates?"

"Willie thinks the *Sea Wolf* is smuggling stowaways from China," I told her.

"I never said that! I said *maybe*. And not to worry about it!"

Cassidy laughed for no apparent reason.

"It might not be so funny," Lisa snapped, "if they are carrying human cargo. And they come after us!"

"Why would they come after us?" I asked. We swung our kayak around to face the wind. A loon flew by, low above the water, like it was on a mission.

"Hold it now, mates," Roger said. "Aren't we getting ahead of ourselves? This is all just speculation."

"Geez! Don't you think we should get moving?" I said. "If they are smugglers, we're just sitting ducks here!"

"You guys are freaking me out! Knock it off!" said Lisa, who, until now, had almost never been afraid of anything. Last year—white-water rafting, almost bit by a rattler—Lisa never showed fear. But now it was as if the unknown had been given a face:

The face of the man with the eyes of a wolf.

"There's nothing to be scared of, Lisa," said Roger, gently. "Like I said, this is all just conjecture."

"Okay," said Willie. "Enough chitchat! Let's roll."

Soon we were all taking off across the waves again.

* * *

Terns, auklets, murres, black oystercatchers—Roger named each bird as it winged and darted and dove in the watery world around us. As if there wasn't a care in the world.

No smugglers. No pirates. No sea captains haunting my dreams.

Finally, we slid along a rocky island rimmed with

stunted spruce right down to the shoreline. Roger, Willie, and Dad scanned with their binos for a good place to camp.

Nothing.

We'd been lucky finding good spots to camp—and we'd been lucky with the weather, too. Now, as we punched into the wind, there was no place in sight. Tomorrow, Roger had said, we'd make the run across Tide Rip Pass to Goose Island, out in the open Pacific. Tonight we needed a good night's rest.

Just when I thought my arms were going to fall out of their sockets from all the paddling we'd been doing, we ducked into a tiny hidden inlet and found a place to pull in.

The tide was out, and we had to haul our kayaks a long way over sharp stones. My feet kept slipping in my wet water sandals, and I wished I were wearing water boots, like Roger, Cassidy, and Willie.

We tied off and went scouting for places to camp. The dwarf forest was so dense that we had to fight our way around. But we soon came upon some big cedars, and there at their feet were what we were looking for: flat beds of soft needles.

Even from here we could hear the barnacles in the tide pools clicking and hissing. Or was it our stomachs?

"I'm starved," I said.

"The sea is your garden," Roger said. "What are you waiting for?"

Even before making camp, we all scrambled down over

the rocks and started rummaging around for something edible.

Willie pulled out his bowie knife—a large hunting knife—and tugged limpet snails off the beach rocks by slipping his blade between shell and rock. He scooped out small chunks of white meat and popped them into his mouth. "Sea popcorn!" he said with a hearty laugh.

"Escargot," Roger said, scooping one into his mouth. "Snails seasoned with sea salt. Nothin' better."

"Dude! Let's start a fire and cook up some real food," Cassidy snarled.

Lisa laughed. "The he-man doesn't eat at the sushi bar, huh?" She held out her hand for a couple of chunks of raw snail from Roger and tossed one into her mouth. "Deee-lish-ious," she said in a refined English accent. "Won't you try one, Cassidy, dear?" she added, holding one out to him.

"Not me!" said Cassidy, shaking his head, and he went scouting down in a tide pool, looking for oysters or clams. Food you could barbecue over an open fire.

"I'll try one," I said.

But Lisa, teasing me, popped it into her mouth and chewed slowly, going mmm-yummm—like it was the tastiest morsel in the world. She licked her lips and made big eyes at me.

Why is she doing this? I wondered, though I guess I knew the answer. She just took pleasure in teasing me. Or torturing me.

But why?

I fished out my Swiss Army knife, pulled out the small blade, and plucked my own snail. Gulped raw, it was like chewing a gritty raw oyster, only a little tougher.

I can't say I really loved it.

* * *

Hunger no longer made my stomach rumble. But something else did.

Was it the raw limpet snails?

Or was it buried fear twisting my intestines?

I didn't know. I hauled our gear up and helped set up the tent and helped look for driftwood, and tried to quell whatever it was making my belly hurt. Making my throat feel like there was a large clam stuck in there. Still in its shell. A geoduck.

* * *

After dinner we sat around the fire as the first stars came out, one by one, like pinpricks of doubt. I kept thinking about the "pirates," and who might be stowed in the hold of their boat.

I felt like I needed a little space, especially from the adults, so I got up and wandered away. Nobody said anything. I just walked farther down the beach.

But when I sat down and leaned against a drift log, along came Lisa and Cassidy. They sat down beside me, Lisa next to me, Cassidy on her other side, facing the sea.

I didn't mind. Not really. Though it would've been better if it was just Lisa.

Then out of the blue, I started talking about what I'd been thinking. "The man on the *Sea Wolf*, the captain, did you notice he was trying to get that diver to hurry into the fishing boat? Like he didn't want him to talk to us. And he must know we heard that cry coming from inside his boat. What if he figures out we know there's something not right going on inside that boat. If he really is smuggling stowaways, he won't want to be found out. He'll come after us."

"I'll be ready if they do," Cassidy said, folding his thick arms across his chest.

"Oh my God," said Lisa. "You should listen to yourself. You're going to do battle with the bad guys and save us all."

"Where I live," I said, trying to change the subject, but not too much, "migrant workers stand on street corners in the morning, trying to get work. Our neighbors sometimes hire them when they need help: building fences, cleaning gutters, digging gardens. Everybody pretty much assumes that most of them crossed the border from Mexico illegally."

"I've read about migrants from Mexico, and Central America, too," said Lisa, getting into the conversation now, "paying 'coyotes' to sneak them across the border. They're always trying to squeeze more money out of the migrants, using threats to their families and making slaves of the ones who don't pay."

"Yeah," Cassidy cut in. "I've seen that on TV, too. Sometimes the coyotes run off with the money and leave 'em locked in the backs of trucks in the hot sun. US border guards find a truck in the desert, open the door, and—whoa! pile of dead bodies inside."

"That's gross," Lisa said, hugging her knees. "And evil."

The image of those bodies burned in my mind. Were there really people trapped in the bottom of that fishing boat? "If that boat we saw capsized and sank with refugees inside, they'd all go down with it, and drown."

"Yeah. The coyotes and . . . what did Willie call them? *Snakeheads?* They should all be shot," Cassidy said. "Or at least thrown in jail. When I was in juvie, some of the guys I know were from Mexico. They told some bad stories about coyotes. I felt kinda sorry for them I guess, but they had no business being here in the first place. They would've been better off staying at home. And they were taking our jobs. They were taking my job! I had to compete with them to get a lousy job at a McDonald's! And my best bud, Ronnie, he's a Spokane Indian. A real native American, not an immigrant. And he couldn't get a job anywhere, unless he wanted to pick apples with the migrant workers. I don't know. I say we send them all back where they come from, the ones that came in illegally. It would be better in the end for everyone."

"I can't believe you'd have those people you know sent away!" Lisa said. "America, and Canada, too, were totally founded on immigration. My great-great grandparents were Dutch and French and Irish. When the Irish first came here, they weren't allowed in restaurants and stores and cafes in lots of places. The owners would put up signs that said 'No Negroes. No Irish. No dogs.' People hated the Irish. Wanted them to go home, too."

"At least they were white," Cassidy said.

"I can't believe you just said that!" Lisa yelled. "Your best bud, Ronnie, he's not white, right?"

Cassidy didn't say anything. He just looked down, like he was ashamed or something. I was way more on Lisa's side. But it was complicated. I really had to think this through.

"They all just wanted a better life," Lisa said. "That's what our country is built on. And that's what these people coming in now want. It's just human."

"But then they're at the mercy of the human traffickers," Cassidy said. "And those guys are brutal. They'd betray their own mothers if the money was right."

"If more were allowed to come in legally," Lisa said, "fewer would fall into the hands of the human traffickers. We need to fix the laws, that's what I think."

That made sense to me. But it was still complicated. There are a lot of people who can't find jobs. Like librarians. Our school library doesn't even have one anymore. I was about to mention this when Willie came running over, bent low like in a war movie or something.

"Listen," Willie said, stooping down.

"What?" said Cassidy.

"Quiet!"

Then we all heard it. The sound of something splashing through the shallows.

It was coming our way.

CHAPTER NINE

THE ROGUE OF TIDE RIP PASS

Willie pulled a high-powered flashlight from the canvas sack at his feet, flicked it on, and stood up.

The light burned a hole in the night.

The night was still and dark. The waxing moon hid behind the clouds. We walked in a crouch behind Willie through the dense, stunted spruce. It suddenly occurred to me: What if it were smugglers—the crew of the *Sea Wolf*—and what if they were hunting us down? We had no weapons (unless you counted hunting knives)—no way to defend ourselves if they had guns. We should be hiding, not heading unarmed toward whatever was coming.

Willie ducked behind a boulder at the water's edge, and we squatted down beside him as he trained the beam of his flashlight on the star-freckled water. Something big and dark was swimming toward us, across Tide Rip Pass. As it drew closer, we could see a large hump behind a huge head.

"Brown bear!" Willie said.

Cassidy didn't hesitate. He picked up a rock and fired it at the approaching animal. It splashed a few feet short.

"Don't!" I said. "You'll just make it angry!" I remembered Cassidy throwing rocks at the rattlesnake last year, and how if he'd missed, the rattlesnake could've bit Lisa.

But then Willie picked up a stone and lobbed it right at the bear's head.

Soon Roger—and even Dad and Lisa!—were bombarding the poor bear with rocks. I say "poor bear," but I'd read about them. How the huge, coastal brown bears are fast and unpredictable. Big cousins of the grizzly. I picked up a stone, hefted it in my hand, but I just couldn't throw it.

But I held it ready, just in case.

Just then the moon burst through the cloud cover and lit up the bear's big furry face.

It was maybe twenty-five to thirty yards out—about the length of a swimming pool—when it stood up, massive and dripping wet, opened its great jaws, and ROARED at us.

Cassidy and the others stopped firing rocks, and we all jumped back. Then we just stood there, staring at the bear, shrinking back into ourselves.

Finally it snorted and made a huffing sound, then sank back down, turned around, and started swimming the other way, back across Tide Rip Pass.

Cassidy let out a hair-raising howl and yelled, "Adios, old bear!"

"Adios, old bear!" Lisa echoed.

Adios! I said to myself.

There was an eerie silence, just the ripple of the bear

through the water, the slightest wavelets breaking quietly against the rocky shore.

I was just about to question the need to throw stones, when Willie, as if hearing my thoughts, started talking.

"Brown bears can climb trees," Willie said. "I saw them do it in Alaska. If it had come ashore, there'd be no place on this tiny island to hide. And that was a rogue bear; brown bears rarely leave the mainland. It should be on a bank, batting salmon out of a river somewhere. Leave 'em alone and they usually leave you alone. But that rogue was coming toward us. You don't wait to see what happens with a bear like that."

"Not that stones were gonna dent that thick skull of his," Roger said. "But they did turn him back, like a swarm of bees."

Dad patted Cassidy's back and said, "Good job, Cassidy. Quick thinking!" It was like a needle stuck in my skin hearing my dad praise him like that. I couldn't remember the last time he praised me like that. And to think that Dad had actually yelled at Cassidy last year for throwing a rock at the rattler! He'd said it was dangerous and would just make the rattler angry.

And I couldn't help but think, What if it had been smugglers? Throwing rocks wouldn't have done much good against men with guns.

"I've got pepper spray," Lisa said, as if reading my mind. "That ole bear wasn't gonna get in my face!"

* * *

It was hard falling asleep after that. I still felt sorry for the bear, but a little relieved, too.

Back in our tent, I played things over and over. The rogue bear coming. The beating of my heart speeding up. The massive bear standing up so close, I could imagine smelling its breath. Its breath of rotten salmon, crushed mussels by the pawful, and fermenting berries.

I replayed the scene till I couldn't tell if I was dreaming or thinking. It became the stuff of dreams.

* * *

In the morning I was still angry and upset about my dad praising Cassidy, like he'd done the right thing and I'd done the wrong thing. I almost asked Dad about it when we were packing up, but I felt too out of it, and anyway, I didn't know what to say.

I wasn't fully awake until we were in the middle of Tide Rip Pass, heading southwest.

On the ebb tide, tide rips and standing waves challenged us as we hit the juncture of Queens Sound. It was like shooting the rapids in Desolation Canyon, only we were in narrow kayaks instead of wide rafts. Roger had taught me how to brace—holding the paddle flat against the surface and leaning down on it—and had coached us never to allow our kayak to be struck broadside by a wave. But I had to rely on Dad in the cockpit behind me, working the pedals to operate the rudder and steer the boat.

"Whoa!" Willie yelled. "You can flip in this chowder if you don't watch out!" The sea roiled white around us as we struggled to point the prow at a slight angle into each crashing wave. Water seeped down where my spray skirt wasn't drawn tight enough. It was puddling on the seat beneath me—and it was cold.

I paddled like a windmill, racing the speed of my heartbeat. Panic was only kept at bay by the sheer total concentration required to get us through.

At last, about halfway to Goose Island, the McMullin Islets provided shelter. With bald eagles watching down at us from atop the tall trees, we paused and rested, as if we'd just climbed a peak. To the east, in the far distance, were the white-tipped peaks of the great continent of North America; to the west were the waves of the vast Pacific Ocean.

And the smugglers—if that's what they were—were nowhere in sight.

* * *

We munched some gorp, drank lots of water, and set back off into the sea of whitecaps. Dad let me sit in back, working the rudder pedals and steering the kayak. It was super cool! I aimed for the glimmer of white sand topped with dark green that was Goose Island.

At last, when we were just offshore, we aimed straight for the beach, waiting for a good incoming wave, and then paddled like crazy, trying to drive our kayaks right up onto the beach.

"Good job, kiddo!" said Dad. There it was, the first time this trip that he'd said it. I glowed with that for a moment— but just a moment, because I was still mad at him. Then I jumped out and pulled the kayak up before the next surge could wash over us, or the backwash pulled us back out.

I shouted and waved to Lisa as she and Roger pulled their kayak up on the beach. She waved back.

This time Lisa and I just threw our gear up higher on the beach, then took off our footwear and started running.

The beach on the northwestern coast of Goose Island was another stretch of paradise. The sand was pure white, composed of clamshells pulverized by the ocean surf. When we raced across it, the sand squeaked beneath our bare feet, like the squeal of basketball shoes on a gym floor.

Again I held my own against Lisa. She laughed, breathless, face flushed with blood, and flung her arms over my shoulders when we came to a stop. I turned around and kissed her briefly— but almost missed her lips.

Yikes! Did I just do that?

It was almost like another person did that. Someone inhabiting my body. Someone with way more daring than me.

I don't know who was more shocked. It surprised me as much as it surprised her. It wasn't much of a kiss, but it was our first.

Suddenly she laughed, said, "You're crazy!" and ran off down the beach.

I looked over her shoulders. Cassidy was already digging for clams in the wet sand.

* * *

My lips still burning, my heart still soaring like an eagle, we strolled back to the others, not saying a word, just the backs of our hands lightly brushing as our arms swung.

Had we moved on to another level?

I didn't know. And I didn't know what to say. What was I supposed to say? "Hey, wasn't that fun kissing?" She probably would've said something about how clumsy it was, and laughed at me again. I already felt awkward enough without that.

Using small folding camp shovels, we all dug for fresh clams after Cassidy first struck gold.

And in the evening after pulling our kayaks up to the trees, setting up camp, scavenging for driftwood and making a big fire, we ate butter clams, horse clams, bent-nosed clams, and steamers. Cooked by Master Chef Wild Man Willie, it was one of the best meals I've ever had.

We lingered long over the meal. We listened to the washing of the sea as it slid up and down the beach. And looked up at the stars, which seemed to be scrubbing the night with their brightness.

"There's supposed to be an island of ghost bears out here somewhere," Dad said, out of nowhere.

"Ghost bears?" I said. "Seriously? Is this another one of your scary stories?"

"No. There are oral stories about them told by some of the Coastal First Nations, but they are really mutated black bears that live up here somewhere, or maybe farther north on the central and northern coast. They're white, but not albinos. They don't have pink eyes. They're a rare version of a black bear, with a mutant gene. Some people call them ghost bears, or spirit bears. They haunt a mist-shrouded island somewhere along this coast.

"Right on!" Cassidy said. "An island of Teenage Mutant Bears!"

Nobody laughed. There was something way too mysterious and haunting about ghost bears to joke about.

But it did lead to some ghost stories.

And we stayed up so late telling scary stories that we watched the tide come in and drown the fire at our feet! Seriously! We watched as it flickered out and bubbles of seawater burst into steam.

Then we laughed as we jumped up, collecting our stuff and backing off from the incoming tide.

Finally, we crawled into our tents, our hearts and bellies full.

We'd made camp well up in the trees, because the wind off the open ocean can blow an empty tent clear out to sea.

Plus we didn't want to be spotted by the *Sea Wolf* if it came looking for us.

But I wasn't ready to sleep. I sat at the mouth of our tent, scraping sand off my feet, and listening in the dark.

I couldn't stop thinking about that kiss. Even bumbled as it was, it still burned on my lips, like the heat of the fire before the tide came in and drowned it out.

Dad was already snoring like a walrus. I made up my mind.

I hopped up and stepped in the dark toward Roger and Lisa's tent. I hoped she'd come out so we could talk—and maybe even . . . you know . . . other stuff.

But then I heard laughter coming from Cassidy's tent. It sounded like Lisa.

Bummer.

I hesitated, burning with jealousy.

Then, trying to overcome it, I crept over to Cassidy's tent and said, "Knock knock," and ducked my head in. They looked up, startled. They were playing cards, seated cross-legged, facing each other.

"Hey," I said, trying to sound cool. "Can I join ya?"

"Sure, dude. If you wanna play strip poker," Cassidy said deadpan. They both stared at me. But then Lisa let out a shriek and rolled over laughing.

"That was hilarious!" said Cassidy. "He's all, like, whaaaaa?"

Suddenly the loud throb and hum of a boat cut him short. Cassidy threw back the tent flap. A powerful spotlight was sweeping the beach.

Through the trees we saw the silhouette of a large fishing boat cruising the shore.

The *Sea Wolf.*

CHAPTER TEN

THE *SEA WOLF*

Cassidy swore. Lisa grabbed my arm—or did I grab hers? The *Sea Wolf* moved slowly against the low stars. How did they know we were here?

The smoke from our fire!

They must have seen it from miles away. Luckily the fire had long been drowned by the tide, and our kayaks were drawn up into the forest, hidden from the sea.

We held still. Silent. The boat rose and fell with the swells and motored slowly down the beach.

I was about to relax when it turned around, just beyond the surf, and the spotlight slid across the sand again.

But even if they wanted to, how could they land their fishing boat in this surf?

The answer soon came. They dropped anchor—maybe two soccer fields away down the beach and about half that far out—and lowered a dinghy from their stern deck. Three men climbed into it, and one manned the oars and pointed the small boat toward shore.

It bobbed through the surf, and for a moment I thought it would capsize. But whoever handled it knew what he was doing. When they were close enough, in the backwash of the rollers, all three men managed to scramble out and splash ashore. Above them, a bone-white moon floated toward the west.

I gasped. Each man held a weapon at the ready: one a rifle, the other two spearguns. Moonlight glinted off the metal.

Proof! I thought. Proof of what I had thought all along: these were bad guys. Smugglers. My whole body clenched up. How do you breathe when it feels like life as you know it is about to end?

When life, period, is about to end?

The three men stopped halfway up the beach, then split up. One of the speargun men headed down the beach; the other two came toward us.

The two men with spearguns flicked on flashlights at the same time, walking in opposite directions. The leader gripped his rifle, sweeping it side to side, sighting through an ultraviolet scope, which would make his targets glow in the dark.

Cassidy swore again, crouching down beside me. Lisa said nothing, but I could hear her grinding her teeth.

I thought of the Swiss Army knife in my pants pocket. I thought of Lisa's pepper spray.

And I thought about how they would do against two spearguns and a rifle.

My heart raced, but time stood still.

"We have to tell our dads!" Lisa said.

"Quiet!" Cassidy said. It was a small explosion of a whisper. "No time! And the dads were kinda expecting this. They just didn't want to scare you. We don't want to be in this tent when those guys find it. We have to get away or we won't be any use to our dads. We can handle this!"

"Yeah," I said. "We can handle this!" I didn't want to sound scared, but I was. And angry, too. The "dads" told Cassidy that they expected this, but they didn't tell me or Lisa.

But at the same time, I felt relieved. If they expected this, maybe they were ready for it.

Cassidy had snatched his fishing knife and crawled out. He'd been sent to juvie for smashing a man's head with a baseball bat, so I knew he wouldn't be afraid to use it.

But I wasn't so sure about what good it would be against three armed pirates with murder in their hearts.

"*Go go go go!*" hissed Cassidy, commando-style. We burst out of the tent and followed Cassidy into the woods.

Twigs snapped underfoot like the bones of small animals.

Cassidy moved silently through the brush, low and lean. I tried to move like him. As much as his attitude often bothered me, it was good to have him on your side.

"Over here!" Willie hissed. He was crouched behind a thick old cedar. "I was about to come and warn you. Follow me!"

We stepped like deer through the windfall branches,
carefully, carefully. A light beam bounced down along the
beach, not fifty yards away. It rippled through the trees, and
we froze in our tracks.

My heart pounded, echoing the pounding of the sea. My
intestines twisted into a tangle of kelp. I held my breath.

We all held our breath.

Then the beam advanced along the beach, away, and we
all breathed out in unison.

A little deeper into the trees, we linked up with Roger and my dad (I was almost embarrassed at how glad I was to see him), and together we continued on toward the interior of the island.

Cassidy stopped for a moment and turned around, raising his fishing knife, like the thin blade of moonlight sliding through the trees. "If they get too close, I know what to do with this knife!"

I winced at the thought of it. Mr. Macho Man. But at the

same time I felt glad again that he was right beside me, and not against me. We needed everything going for us to get out of this in one piece.

Or we'd get out of this in several pieces.

* * *

We all hid inside the burnt-out base of a giant red cedar and sunk into ourselves, into our shells, as quiet as turtles. No one spoke. We just listened.

The sound of the surf, muffled by trees. The sound of our breathing.

Barely.

Lisa was pressed against my side, but my mind hardly registered it. It, too, had dwindled down to a pinpoint of fear. A pearl of terror.

The tentacle of time stretched slowly around our throats, and squeezed.

But nobody came. No light burst into our little womb in the tree. Our cedar cave. No gun blasted the night wide open.

After an hour, or three, we crept back out, through the trees and to the edge of the beach.

The *Sea Wolf* was gone.

The moon shone down.

"'A vast radiant beach, and a cool jeweled moon,'" Dad said.

"Shakespeare?" Willie looked at the moon.

"Jim Morrison," said Dad. "The Doors."

"Dad and his 'golden oldies.'" I rolled my eyes. Dad was always quoting rhymes from dead singers or poets.

We were exhausted from lack of sleep, but Willie wanted to embark at dawn. "We have to get out of here," he said. "The crew of the *Sea Wolf* coming after us with weapons is proof that they're smugglers, or at least up to no good. They'll be back."

There it was. All spelled out. My thoughts exactly!

Willie's plan was to start early and head south along the coast of Goose Island and to round the southern tip before the wind picked up. This would be our one run in unprotected ocean, and once we rounded the southern tip, the beginning of our return northeast, back toward Bella Bella.

We all pitched in and did what Willie told us: we gathered dry wood with no cones or needles attached for Willie to make a smokeless fire.

Dad and I stooped down and grabbed the same chunk of driftwood at the same time. We held each end in a tense silence. We looked into each other's eyes and it was as if I transmitted my feelings of betrayal to him for trusting Cassidy with the truth and not me. I could see in his eyes that Dad knew he had hurt me, but also that he didn't know what to do about it.

Dad let go and I brought the wood to the fire Willie had started. He put the kettle on.

When it was ready, we drank hot coffee and waited for the sun to rise.

"Man!" said Cassidy, breaking the silence. "That was pretty sick, playing commandos versus smugglers."

"It's no game," Dad said. "They're dead serious."

"Well, mate," said Roger, "you could call it a game of cat and mouse."

"I'd rather be a cat than a mouse," said Lisa.

* * *

Dawn rose out of the east. Soon it was time to break camp and get underway.

Just before we set off, Roger found a green glass ball washed up on the beach. He said it had come from a Japanese fishing boat that had lost its net or capsized in a storm at sea. The glass ball was beautiful, in an antique sort of way, but it struck me as a bad omen.

Probably because I couldn't get the image of a capsized Japanese fishing boat out of my head.

Just as the sun pierced the clouds to the east, we set off through the breakers and paddled out—in the direction of Japan—then turned south. Dad and I were almost perfectly synchronized. I'd learned to twist my torso with each stroke, bracing my legs against the hull and my feet against the bottom, putting my whole body into it, rather than putting all the strain on my arms and shoulders.

At first the sea was relatively calm, but the wind picked up early, and soon we were riding the deep swells of the open Pacific Ocean. It was an awesome feeling, slowly rising and sinking, on the rising and falling chest of the ocean.

Within the hour we were hit by offshore boomers—waves breaking unexpectedly far out at sea. With the waves towering over us, we almost lost each other in the valleys between swells. We'd rise to the crest, shout and wave and get our bearings, then slide back down to the bottom.

WHAM! We were slammed by a gray wall of water.

Then we rose up and careened down the face of a big roller, rose up again, and slid back down another white-crested mountain of thunder. My stomach rose to my mouth as we plummeted down yet another wave.

At the top of the next peak, Roger pointed toward shore.

"Head further in!" he shouted.

His words were snatched away by the next crashing wave—and within seconds . . .

. . . Dad and I were flipping over.

We were capsizing!

CHAPTER ELEVEN

THE ROOT PEOPLE

Brace!" Dad yelled. We dug our paddle blades into the breaking wave and held them flat, parallel to the water, leaning into them, pressing down. Sliding sideways, hanging at a precarious angle, I held my breath and concentrated on staying afloat.

And alive.

We were almost swamped—water having leaked in through our spray skirts—but didn't give in, and finally managed to push ourselves upright.

A little here and a little there, Roger had trained us well.

We caught sight of the other kayaks, then paddled hard and fast, back toward Goose Island.

We were west of the beach now; rock cliffs met the ocean here. And that created a new problem: waves that boomed against the cliffs, then rolled back through the ocean waves that were coming in, causing enormous standing waves to erupt. Just like the "haystacks" we ran into in the river rapids in Desolation Canyon last year. And the closer we got to the cliffs, the more the sea surged outward between the swells.

"Go with the surge!" Roger shouted. "Don't fight it! The next incoming wave might crash you on the rocks!"

Suddenly a haystack wave erupted beneath us and tossed us in the air—like a killer whale tossing a sea lion. We smacked down on our side and I thought, This is it!

But a frantic low brace pushed us back upright again, and Dad and I paddled on.

We slid back out with each surge, but battled on, until we were in a safer zone of rolling swells.

Lisa flashed a smile and waved from the next crest, while Cassidy hollered, "Rock 'n' ROLL!"

* * *

At last, we rested in the lee of Goose Island, out of the wind. We sloshed around, slumped in our kayaks, exhausted and hungry. We dug our hands into bags of gorp, and glanced up at circling, squawking seagulls and shrieking bald eagles.

Since the ferry wouldn't be back to Bella Bella to pick us up for four more days, we needed a plan for avoiding the *Sea Wolf*.

We closed in and formed a sea huddle. After Roger and Willie pored over the charts, it was decided to hide out among the islets and lagoons for the next few days, then shoot up Hunter Channel to Bella Bella in time to catch the ferry.

"Number one," Willie said, "is not to let the *Sea Wolf*

find us. That means smokeless fires, hugging the shore as much as possible, and no broad daylight paddles across wide-open passages."

Geez, it was one bummer after another, but nobody said anything. We were too busy focusing our energy on surviving.

We'd have to start across Queens Sound at dusk. It was a long ocean passage, and we were afraid of getting caught by a tidal rip in the dark.

We paddled into shore and broke up into two groups.

Roger and Dad—keeping watch for the *Sea Wolf*—went back out together and trawled for salmon not far offshore. The rest of us pulled our kayaks in among the boulders below the cliffs, and tied them off. Then we hunted the tide pools for sea bounty.

No matter what, we needed food. Long hours of paddling took super amounts of energy. And there were no supermarkets out here.

Willie gathered purple sea urchins, bristling with needles. Lisa and I plucked mussels from the rock walls. And Cassidy—after changing into a wet suit, with snorkel, mask, and fins—free dived for huge purple hen scallops.

And on his last dive, he came up dangling a long, ugly salami with warts: a sea cucumber.

"A delicacy, dude," Cassidy said, dangling it over his mouth. As long as it wasn't raw, he'd eat anything.

And I knew, if we got hungry enough, so would Lisa and I.

Our stomachs were growling but there was no time to make a fire and cook our bounty.

With our stash—and the one medium-sized salmon Dad and Roger had caught—we started across Queens Sound as the sun and wind stirred the clouds into a broth of gold, pink, and gray.

To cut wind resistance, we feathered our paddles against the wind, spinning the forward blade horizontal, slicing into the wind with each stroke.

And we kept our eyes peeled for the *Sea Wolf*.

By dark we'd crossed the sound and found a hidden cove on the lee of a tiny island. We pulled our kayaks well out of view among the trees and pitched our tents at the foot of cedars. Then we scavenged the beach for driftwood, and Willie built a small, almost smokeless fire.

The black sky folded its raven wings around us.

Willie cooked yet another seafood feast, which we ate in silence. Lisa got up and came back with a book. All I could make out in the firelight was the cover. Something about totem poles, with a picture of one. She started to read, but I think it was too dark. She put it down.

I was going to ask her about it—and tell her about the one I was reading, about Mt. Everest—but the sudden image of Chinese immigrants stowed in the hull of the *Sea Wolf* haunted my mind.

"Dad?" I said, leaning back against a log. "You told me

once that the migrant workers send most of their money to their families back in Mexico, or wherever. Is that what the Chinese do?"

Dad rubbed his fuzzy jaw. "I think so, Aaron. But all I know for sure is they're desperate to flee China—desperate enough to risk their lives."

I chewed on that for a bit. It's like what Lisa had said, about them wanting "a better life." The sea breeze stirred the trees.

"You're young," Dad said after awhile, "looking out at a big world through little eyes. Trying to make sense of it."

"Really, Dad? I'm thirteen, you know." This really gets to me. He talks to Cassidy like he's a man, but to me, it's like I'm still a kid.

"I didn't mean it that way, but you are, well. . . . "

"What? A little boy? Is that what you're saying, Dad?"

He threw a chunk of wood into the fire, and for a moment it flared up, throwing sparks against the sky.

Lisa stood up and walked off alone toward her tent. Cassidy got up and followed her. Jealousy tugged my string again, pulled it tight, like a bow.

"You left your book, Lisa," I said, but I don't think she heard me. I started to get up, to follow them. Then sat back down. I didn't want to go uninvited. To act like a stalker. Dad got up and dished himself more food, then came back and sat down beside me again, perching his metal plate on a bony knee.

"How ya holding up, kiddo?"

I shrugged.

"Food's good, right?" he said.

I gave him a thumbs-up.

"Miss Mom? Your brother?"

I shrugged again.

A little whisper told me: he's trying. But I was trying, too. I just didn't know what to say. Thoughts of the *Sea Wolf*, smuggled immigrants, Lisa and Cassidy hanging out together, scrambled around in my mind like crabs, snapping their nasty little claws.

Finally, Dad got up, stretched his back, and strolled off to clean his plate.

Ten minutes later, Lisa stumbled back toward the fire and dropped down, clutching herself. She looked angry.

I knew it, I thought. Cassidy must've said something or done something to make her mad.

"Where's Cassidy?" Willie asked.

"Like I care," Lisa snapped. She picked up her book on totems, then immediately dropped it back down.

The tree branches creaked, and the sea boomed and sizzled.

"It's time for a story!" Roger said, trying to sound jolly.

"And I know one," said Dad. In fact, he knew lots of stories. He sat by the fire, a steaming cup of tea balanced on his knee. "It's a Tlingit story. The Tlingit people live just north of here, up on the Alaskan panhandle."

"Just tell the story, Dad." Sometimes I loved his stories. Other times I wished he'd just shut the heck up.

"Well," Dad said, taking a sip of hot tea, "long ago, river otters were called Kuschtas, meaning 'Root People,' because they lived among the roots of trees. The Root People could change into humans and back into otters at will. And though they weren't big and ferocious like bears, they were feared even more than bears or wolves."

He let the silence seep into our bones. The flames flung their dancing shadows against the trunks of the trees.

"The Root People were tricksters," he continued. "They'd approach near-drowning victims in their capsized canoes, disguised as humans, and lend a helping hand. But then they'd kidnap them and drag them, kicking and scream-ing, back to their villages, where their captives, too, would turn into Root People. Lost forever to their families back home."

This reminded me of the Water Babies, another scary story Dad told last year in Desolation Canyon.

"Is that it? Is that the end of the story?" Lisa asked.

"What I remember of it," Dad said, grinning.

"Well, according to this book I'm reading," she said, "the stories of the First Nations usually have a little more point to them," she said, smiling. "The tribes up here carved totems of otters and ravens and killer whales and other ani-mals to represent their clans and family histories. One story I read was about how humans who drown in the sea become

killer whales and that's why they never hurt people, even though they're hunters. They might even try to help them, like dolphins do."

"Thanks for that, Lisa," Roger said. "I'd like to take a look at that book of yours sometime. But I'm bushed; now it's time for some shut-eye." He flung what was left of the tea in his cup into the sand, said goodnight, and headed for their tent.

"I think tomorrow we rest," Willie said. "Then take off at sunset and paddle across the channel under the cover of darkness."

"What about we go look for one of these burial islands?" Lisa said, picking up her book.

She flipped through some pages, then showed us a photo of a burial island with some totem poles on it. "Mortuary totems," she said. "This island is supposed to be around here somewhere. We could probably get there and back in just a couple of hours, with time to check it out. That would be so awesome!"

She flipped to another page. It was a map, showing a tiny burial island east of us, over toward Hunter Island. I couldn't make out its name in the firelight.

Willie grinned but shook his head. "No can do, Lisa. Sorry. We need the rest. We're gonna need all the energy we can muster tomorrow evening. And remember, we're supposed to be lying low, with the *Sea Wolf* out there somewhere."

"But this is our last chance!" Lisa said.

Willie just shrugged and shook his head again.

Lisa slapped her book against her thigh, looked at me like maybe she was hoping I'd say something, then got up and went to her tent.

I felt like I let her down, but maybe Willie was right. With smugglers out there and all.

The fire was slowly shutting down, and with it, the night.

Dad and I stood up at the same time. "After you, Aaron," he said. I skipped brushing my teeth and ducked right into our tent. I was too exhausted to even get out of my clothes.

I crawled into my sleeping bag, and listened to the sea slapping the sand silly. I tried not to think about the Root People, or even killer whales. I tried not to listen to my dad snoring, moments after his head hit the pillow. I tried to fall into the oblivion of sleep.

And when I finally did, I dreamt about Chinese immigrants huddled in the bowels of a ship with their ankles shackled like slaves. They moaned in pain. A hatch opened and light poured down on a girl's face.

But she wasn't Chinese. It was Lisa, her eyes wide with terror.

* * *

In the morning, Dad was up already when I opened my eyes. Something was wrong. I could feel it.

I shimmied out of my sleeping bag and waddled out into the mist barefooted, my mind groggy with sleep. And followed the sound of voices.

There they were, staring out into the cove.

"What's going on?" I asked nobody in particular.

"We can't find Lisa," Willie said. "She's gone. Missing. She took off in their kayak and hasn't come back."

Lisa's missing? Lisa's missing!

My first irrational thought was of the Root People. She was kidnapped by the Root People.

Then my mind came awake.

My next thought was of the *Sea Wolf* and the smugglers— traffickers in human cargo.

And Lisa was out there, alone, at their mercy.

CHAPTER TWELVE

THE SKULL

"LISA!" Roger called, his hands cupping his mouth. An osprey crashed into the cove, lifting off with a salmon clutched in its sharp talons.

She'd gone to sleep beside her dad in their tent, but when he woke up, she was gone.

Roger called again. Shreds of mist hung like skin from the branches, slashed with spears of sunlight.

"Did she say anything last night?" Dad asked. "She seemed upset."

"Nothing." Roger pulled on his water boots; the usual twinkle in his eye was buried like a blackened coal. "We've got to find her."

"Cassidy," Willie said, snapping a stick for kindling. "What happened between you two last night?"

"Nothing happened. Chillax." He was leaning against a tree, wrapped in his mummy bag.

Yeah, sure, I said to myself. He couldn't keep his hands off her, is what happened. Or he said something that freaked her out.

But something else nagged my mind. Would she have gone looking for one of those burial islands she'd talked about? Alone?

I didn't think so, but I didn't know.

Roger ran back into the trees, then dragged Willie's kayak out to the waterline. I said, "Dad? I'll take our kayak. Two of us in separate kayaks have a better chance of finding her." I wanted to find her. I needed to find her. Me. I couldn't put into words—even to myself—why this was so, exactly. It was an impulse. I was driven.

Dad scratched his stubbly chin. His blue eyes shone deeper than the sea, and he looked haggard, as skinny as a scarecrow. "Maybe Cassidy should go, kiddo. He has more—"

"I want to go," I cut in. I stood firm, trying not to tremble.

Dad took a deep breath, then let it out. "Okay, Aaron," he said. "Watch your bow—without my weight in front, it'll ride up and catch the wind."

Willie, with his usual energy, was already getting a smokeless fire started. He asked Cassidy to gather wood. "Pronto!"

"Whatever," said Cassidy. Then he slipped out of his mummy bag and let it drop at his feet.

"I'll scout along the shoreline," Dad said, setting off on his own.

Roger was already slicing through the water as I climbed into my kayak. I drew the spray skirt tight and pushed off toward him.

"Wait up!" Cassidy hollered. "I'm comin' with you!" He was only dressed in his boxers, and I saw the tattoos on his pecs flex.

He just wants to be a hero, I thought. "Too late!" I yelled over my shoulder, and paddled like a windmill.

Maybe I just wanted to be a hero, too. But I wasn't thinking.

I was just paddling. Hard and fast.

Soon I was out of the cove, finding my rhythm through the sea.

Dad had said these islands were once the world of the Haida, Tsimshian, Tlingit. He said they were a sea people, paddling dugout canoes and living off the sea.

Lisa had said, before I'd even seen her book, that these people were still here, and up in Alaska, and down along the Washington coast, often on the islands—mostly fishing in modern boats, but some of them still hewing dugout canoes from red and yellow cedar. She said that their traditional burial islands dotted these waters, and that the spirits of their ancestors still lingered here. Like mist, I thought. Or the ever-present bald eagles, always watching from the trees.

And I thought of Lisa with her book of totems. Yes, this is what she was talking about last night. Maybe she would go look for one alone, after all. She wasn't afraid of kayaking alone, and she was angry about not getting a chance to see what she'd been reading about.

And she seemed to be angry at Cassidy, too. . . .

Roger circled back to me, his red bandana blazing in the sun.

"She could be on any one of these islands." He nodded toward a scattering of tree-clad islets to the north and west. Far off to the east, the snowcapped mountains of the mainland were almost lost in the mist.

"Maybe she's exploring that burial island she showed us last night." I said, hopeful. "She really wanted to go see one."

"I missed that," Roger said. "But I could hear her talking

about it. She's a strong kayaker, and yeah, she's super into these cultures, but. . . ." He shook his head.

"I was closest to her," I said. "I could see a map that pointed out a burial island not too far from here. I couldn't read the name, but it was over toward Hunter Island. East."

Roger took a deep breath and looked out in that direction. Hunter Island was huge and still far off, but between it and us there were a couple of green dots. Small islands.

"Okay, mate," Roger said. "Let's go take a look." He turned his kayak and paddled off.

I followed, but had a hard time keeping up. I had to sit in the rear cockpit so I could operate the rudder pedals, and like my dad warned, that caused the bow to rise up and catch the wind. I struggled to stay on course, and at the same time I scanned the horizon for Lisa's kayak.

And the *Sea Wolf.*

I heard a loon's high, crazy, yodeling laugh and looked around. Sure enough, one was floating some twenty yards away. It watched me with its red eyes. A lone loon. Perhaps lost.

Like Lisa, I thought.

The sun was bright. It pierced our eyes. We squinted, and paddled.

We were searching. Hunting. Hoping.

I got a second wind and managed to catch up to Roger, and then pass him.

It was getting dusky. We'd been paddling all afternoon,

in and out of coves, around the two small islands between us and Hunter Island.

Fear was a talon in my heart—fear for Lisa. And exhaustion was a haze drawing the darkness closer.

The white head of a bald eagle, glimpsed in the gloom, drew my attention to a hidden cove we'd missed the first time around. "Over there!" I shouted. "A cove! Let's check it out!"

It was our last chance to find Lisa before dark. Adrenalin shot through me like a flaming arrow and I paddled like crazy.

I was first to round the point and coasted in.

And there it was. Lisa's kayak! It was drifting away on the flood tide.

Empty!

Like an empty coffin waiting for a body.

We coasted, frantically looking for Lisa, calling her name. "LIIISAAA! *LIIIISAAAA!*"

The sun was setting in a blaze of clouds. "Spread out!" I yelled.

We spread out. I headed for the rocks that hugged the shore.

And there she was!

I paddled up to her. She was sprawled on her back on a boulder slick with algae, her eyes closed. The freezing water was lapping against her; one arm was floating limp, like a dead sea snake.

A surge of panic rose in me, but I forced it back down.

Is she dead, or just knocked out?

"Over here!" I shouted. "She's over here!"

I snatched the bowline of her drifting kayak, then skimmed mine ashore and nosed it up to the trees, and pulled hers in. I jumped out—not bothering to tie the kayaks off—and something thumped and rolled to my feet. I stopped in my tracks and looked down.

A human skull.

Covered with moss. Its eye hollows—scooped out of darkness—staring up at me.

CHAPTER THIRTEEN

BURIAL ISLAND

I stepped over the fallen skull, and, still shocked, stared up into the carved face of a killer whale. A weathered, ancient mortuary totem leaned toward me from the trees. Along with Killer Whale, Bear and Raven stared out at me, eaten by salt and wind and time. Just like the totems I'd seen in Lisa's book.

I scrambled over slippery rocks toward her, and got there just before Roger. He knelt and felt her neck.

"She's alive!" Roger said. "Help me here!"

Lisa's *alive!* I thought. I looked back at the carved face of the killer whale, and I remembered what she'd said last night about killer whales saving people from drowning.

Thanks, Killer Whale! I said to myself, feeling mystically foolish.

Roger was still kneeling over her, gently feeling her neck and scalp. She was limp, unconscious. Her face white, drained of blood. The icy cold water lapped up against her.

Her blue shorts were wet, and so were one arm, half her tank top, and most of her hair.

Crows bounced around back in the shadows.

"She's out. I can't seem to wake her," Roger said. "We have to get her back to camp. There's a big knot on her head, but there's no blood, and I don't think anything's broken. What I'm worried about is hypothermia. We have to get her back to a fire and a warm sleeping bag. *Now!* Or we could lose her."

Lose her? Tears seared my eyes, but I forced them back. Tears wouldn't help. Panic wouldn't help. She needed action. I lifted Lisa while Roger cradled her head and back, keeping her spine as straight as possible.

We had no choice but to seat her in the forward cockpit of Roger's reclaimed kayak. He carefully wrestled her into a Gortex raincoat, then adjusted her life jacket so it rode up in back and supported her head. He secured her by stuffing half-filled dry bags from the rear and forward hatches all around her in the cockpit.

Then he kissed her on her forehead and said, "You'll be all right, sweetheart." She looked like she was sleeping.

Roger settled into the rear cockpit and I tied the kayak Roger had borrowed to the back of it, and shoved them off. Then I climbed in mine, shoved off, and paddled out of the hidden cove.

Roger had made compass bearings, and though we'd paddled much of the day looking for Lisa, our camp was probably only about a mile away as the crow flies.

Along the gray horizon to the west spread a thin stain, the color of blood.

* * *

It was almost total dark by the time Dad, Willie, and Cassidy met us in the cove. Lisa was still out cold, and Willie—built like a barge—squatted down, lifted her dead weight out of the kayak, and carried her up to the fire.

Roger ran to his tent and came back with their sleeping bags.

"I'll have to warm her up with my body heat so she doesn't go into hypothermia," Roger said, zipping their bags together. "If she wakes up, I'll move her back to the tent." Deep lines I'd never noticed before creased his face.

Above us the stars came out, one by one, as if from hiding. The waxing moon was well up, hogging their space. The fire crackled and the waves lapped. Willie helped Roger get Lisa into the zipped together bags, then Roger slid in beside her.

Cassidy and Dad gathered driftwood, built a big fire, and helped start dinner boiling in pots on a blackened grill. Willie rigged up a lean-to to keep the heat in.

When it was ready, I helped myself to some soup, but put it down in the sand beside me.

Roger waved away the steaming bowl that Dad held out. He jostled Lisa's arm gently and said, "Wake up, Lisa. It's Dad. Can you hear me?"

I was starving but my stomach had seized up, hard as a skillet.

Finally I picked up the bowl again and sipped some

soup. Roger kept cooing to Lisa, "You'll be okay, sweetheart, you'll be okay."

But would she?

How does Roger know she didn't get water in her lungs? How does he know that she isn't in a coma, dying from hypothermia?

Why doesn't she wake up?

I remembered my dad last year in Desolation Canyon. Unconscious. Dehydrated. With a gash like a second mouth in his forehead. Now here's Lisa, unconscious with a big knot on her forehead, right at the hairline.

After eating as much as I could, I decided to sleep near the fire, too. I unrolled my sleeping bag and climbed in.

Worry over Lisa kept me awake for a long time. Until sleep, like an ebbing tide, finally took me away.

* * *

Lisa woke in the middle of the night, moaning, and it woke me up.

You cannot guess how relieved I was!

No coma. Conscious enough to moan. Not dying. Not dead.

Willie was still tending the fire. Roger said to him, "Take a break, Willie."

Willie crawled into his tent, next to the one where I could hear Cassidy snoring. I brought Roger a bottle of water for Lisa, and offered to help him move her into their tent. He made a tired grin and said, "I got this. We'll go in when she's ready. She's tough, so it shouldn't be long."

I decided to stay out by the fire, and didn't hear them get up during the night.

I drifted between islands of sleep. Sleep filled with fears—all jumbled together in a chowder of dreams.

* * *

In the morning, Lisa and Roger crawled out of their tent and joined the rest of us (minus Cassidy, who was still asleep) at the morning fire. She had bags beneath her eyes, but otherwise she was almost like new!

I asked her what happened, but Roger jumped in and said, "She left me a note but I didn't see it!"

"I left it right on his pillow!" said Lisa, rolling her eyes.

"It got stuck down in my sleeping back somehow." Roger shrugged.

"Sorry you all had to come after me," said Lisa, her face turning red. "Probably wasn't the smartest thing I ever did."

"So what did the note say," I asked her, not totally satisfied with her story.

She didn't answer at first. Then she got up and said, "Let's go for a walk."

I followed her to a sunny spot on the edge of the beach, and sat down beside her in the sand.

"It's embarrassing," she said. "My note said I woke up before sunrise and couldn't get back to sleep. That I was going to explore one of the nearby islands I'd read about, look for totem poles. That I'd be back by noon. We were supposed to hang out all day anyway, remember? Willie said we would head for the open channel after sunset. So I figured I had plenty of time. Didn't figure I'd slip and knock myself out." Lisa rubbed her forehead. "Stupid, I know."

"Yeah, totally stupid," I said. "You scared the crap out of us!"

In a flash, Lisa's expression shifted from embarrassed to irritated. "Look, Dad already scolded me, so I really don't need to hear it from you. I've been kayaking for years—I know what I'm doing. I didn't want to wake anybody up. And I needed some space. I wanted be on my own for the first time on this trip. I knew you and Cassidy would make fun of me if I brought you along—for geeking out about the totem poles and stuff."

"I wouldn't have made fun of you," I told her. "I think totem poles are really cool."

Lisa beamed. That's all the forgiveness she needed to launch into telling me all about it. "It was totally awesome, Aaron! Paddling over to the burial island, by myself, in the early morning light. So peaceful. And when I got there it was so cool, checking out the totem poles, seeing in person what I'd been reading about. It was amazing! I totally lost track of time! So when I realized how late it was, I ran back to my kayak and the tide had started to come in by then, and I slipped. Must have banged my head. I don't remember anything after that."

"You're lucky you didn't drown when the tide came in!" I said. "And you're lucky you rolled over on your back, or your head would've been down in the water!"

Lisa just rolled her eyes at me and jumped up. "I'm hungry," she said, and started back toward the campfire.

When I got back to camp, Lisa was leaning against the log wrapped in her sleeping bag again. I poured her a cup of hot cocoa and held it out to her.

She looked at me for a moment, then took the cup from my hands. "Thanks," she said, and gave me a smile that flew right through me, like a laughing loon.

I went and got myself some hot cocoa, then came back and sat beside her.

"Thanks for finding me, Aaron." She rubbed the bump on her head, now buried in a mess of hair as shiny and black as a raven's feathers. I wished Dad had heard her say it, but he was off fiddling with our kayak.

My heart swelled with pride anyway. "Better thank your dad and . . . and Cassidy, too," I said.

"Cassidy?" she blurted. Then she lowered her voice. "Cassidy is the main reason I wanted to be on my own in the first place! He was bugging me to go swimming with him the other night, and I didn't want to. He was a jerk!"

A kingfisher darted by, on a date with a fish.

I was about to feel all bent out of shape about Cassidy

when, right on cue, he crawled out of his tent and said, "Did I hear my name?"

"Yeah," said Lisa. "I said you're a jerk. Drop dead."

"Ouch!" He clutched his chest and mock died, collapsing to the ground. He lay there, sprawled out, dead.

Then he sprung up and walked on his hands, which isn't easy on uneven ground all littered with branches. And he turned that into a back spring and landed back on his feet. "Boom!"

Lisa couldn't help but laugh. And though I felt that usual bee sting of jealousy, I had to laugh, too, which only made it worse.

* * *

Now that Lisa had gone exploring on a burial island, I wanted to go, too. But Willie said we'd have to hide out from the *Sea Wolf* all day, then paddle north up Hunter Channel, under cover of dusk, and find another hidden cove.

Meanwhile, it was a rest day. A day to kick back, chill, and maybe even have some fun.

We munched gorp, read our books, and played cards, but the *Sea Wolf* was always on our minds.

I jotted a few things in my journal—a habit that had begun last year in Desolation Canyon. But I stopped when I saw Cassidy watching me.

He's not a bad guy, I kept reminding myself. He'd certainly proven that last year. As the saying goes, "you can't tell a book by its cover." I'd learned that last year, too. But he doesn't make it easy. Not for me, and not for Lisa. At least this year he was a little easier on my dad.

A little.

When it wasn't Dad's turn to stand lookout, he and I went fishing in the cove from our kayak. We didn't speak much and just enjoyed the glitter of the sun on the wavelets, and the shadows of eagles sliding over us, and the distant boom of the surf.

And after half an hour I hooked a big, long lingcod, which felt as heavy as a boot filled with mud. In fact, I was sure a boot is what I'd hooked, until I finally pulled it up, and the cod hung there above the water, as long as my arm.

It hadn't put up much of a fight, but it was still a struggle to haul in. Dad said it would make a fine dinner for all of us. But it wasn't much praise for such a big fish.

Lisa said, "Sweet!" when she eyed the big cod I'd caught. But we'd have to wait to eat it. Willie didn't want any fires. He didn't want to draw attention to our little camp on the island.

To keep it alive, I left the lingcod on the stringer and tied it off to the back of our kayak, where it dangled in the shallows slowly swishing its tail and working its gills.

Cassidy said, "Hey! Let's play football!" and grabbed at Lisa. She spun away and almost stifled a laugh, but said, "Let's not but say we did."

I don't know what he had in mind to use for a football,

anyway. Maybe my head. Or a skull from the burial island.

I tried to clear my mind of such morbid thoughts. But it wasn't easy. The *Sea Wolf* was out there, and it wasn't going to let us forget.

We broke camp, loaded the kayaks, and set out just as the sun dropped off the edge of the world.

As darkness descended, we heard the scream of an eagle . . .

. . . and the distant roar of a motor.

CHAPTER FOURTEEN

CAT AND MOUSE

We knew that sound by now. It was the sound of dread. And it was coming our way.

The *Sea Wolf* was somewhere behind us, and gaining steadily. Sound travels far out on the water; there was no telling how distant the boat was. Willie raised his paddle, the signal to regroup. Dad and I coasted up to the others.

"This is the plan," Willie said. "We separate—three targets are harder to hit than one—then meet up on Sprague Island after dark. According to the chart, there's a tiny cove tucked into the southeastern corner." He pulled out the chart and pointed out three ways to get to the cove. Then he handed the chart to Roger, who studied it for a moment and handed it to Dad.

The sound of the motor grew louder. "Whistle like a bird when you enter the cove," Willie said, whistling softly by way of example.

I tried whistling. So did Lisa and Cassidy. I thought Cassidy might make some joke, but this wasn't anything to joke about—not even to Cassidy.

"Okay, mate," was all Roger said.

Willie and Cassidy paddled northwest while Roger and Lisa headed northeast. Dad and I went to what he said was due north, sticking to the channel.

I watched Roger and Lisa's kayak until it became a tiny yellow dot against the dark blue sea, and then disappeared.

I looked over my shoulder. The silhouette of a fishing boat, maybe half a mile away, was cutting our way.

"Dad, they're coming! They're catching up!"

"Let's pull toward shore," he said, "and hide out till they pass by." There was a wooded islet off to the right, the east, maybe three hundred yards away.

I never paddled so hard in my life. We synchronized our strokes so our paddles wouldn't clash, and skimmed across the sea like a flying fish. The first stars popped out, and the moon, well along toward full, grew brighter.

We slipped like a shadow up to the rocky shore, just as the *Sea Wolf* pulled even with us, about a quarter of a mile out in the main channel. They were chugging along at maybe ten or twelve knots per hour, sweeping the sea with their spotlight.

They hadn't seen us. *Yet.*

I looped my arm around a low, overhanging branch, and we hid out in the moon shadow, barely breathing. My arm grew as rigid as the branch it was attached to.

We waited till the *Sea Wolf* dwindled to a spot of light in the growing dark, then breathed out through our mouths.

*** * ***

We waited a few more minutes, then pushed off toward Sprague Island in the last shreds of light.

About an hour or two later, Dad whistled softly as we entered the little cove on Sprague Island in the moonlight. I echoed his whistle, then the same whistle floated back to us. We sounded like songbirds with an attitude.

We crawled out of our kayak and hauled it up in among the trees.

Willie had built a small fire beneath a tarp rigged up like a lean-to. "You're just in time, pard," he said to me, and winked. "Bring me that big cod you hauled in. I got me some good hot coals here."

I went back and unhooked the stringer and returned with the still-alive lingcod, slapping against my shin.

"Thanks," said Willie. "I'll have this puppy good to go faster than you can say *Jiminy Cricket!*"

Lisa made room for me on a log. She let her head rest on my shoulder, but just for a moment. Then she went back to huddling over a hot cup of tea, blowing on it. Nobody spoke.

Twenty minutes later—despite the tension we all felt—our mouths watered when Willie pulled the foil-wrapped cod from the coals with his bare hands. He'd done it again. The stars burned, the waves slapped the shore, and the moon poured its white gold down as we ate that big tasty fish with our fingers and moaned in delight.

* * *

Lisa and I stayed up late, lying on a bed of moss and gazing up at the sky. A dark cloud passed across the moon.

"I had a dream about Chinese immigrants the other night," I whispered, and I described it to her. "I don't know how you got into it, Lisa, but dreams are like that, I guess."

"I know, right? Dreams can be weird," she said, barely beyond a whisper. "Sometimes I think they're trying to tell us something. Maybe you were worried about me, Aaron, but you shouldn't be. I can take care of myself."

"Yeah, like you took care of yourself when you paddled off alone and then slipped on a rock and almost got yourself drowned."

I could feel her tense up next to me.

The wild, haunting cry of a loon pierced the night. It almost made me jump.

"I read that native people up here call loons 'rain birds,'" Lisa said, changing the subject. "If you hear one, it means a storm's on the way."

"It's time for bed, lassie. You too, Aaron" It was Roger, whispering. "We're breaking camp before sun up." I'm not sure why we were all whispering. I'm sure even our regular voices couldn't be heard above the pounding of the surf.

But I guess we weren't taking any chances.

Roger went to his tent. I rolled toward Lisa and she rolled toward me. Her high cheekbones caught the moonlight, and I could feel her warm breath on my face. The whole world seemed to stand still.

But Roger quietly but insistently called us again, the moment broke, and we crawled off to our separate tents.

That didn't mean we slept, though. Speaking just for myself, I don't remember sleeping at all, but sometimes it's hard to tell between a waking dream and a real dream. Dad "caught a few winks" as he called it. His snoring went from soft and fuzzy to loud and annoying. I kept socking the pillow I'd made out of my clothes, and tossing back and forth.

There was no getting comfortable. There was no peace. I just lay there on the sharp roots and rocks of the island, like the jagged shards of my consciousness.

* * *

At the first hint of dawn, we all crawled bleary-eyed and feeling broken-boned out of our damp sleeping bags.

Dad and I walked back out toward our kayak, arms loaded with gear. I was right behind him when suddenly he cried out and slipped on a boulder. He fell hard, right on his elbow.

"You okay, Dad?" I dropped the dry bags and knelt down to help him.

"I'm okay, Aaron." He tried to catch his breath. "I guess I banged my elbow pretty bad, but I don't think I broke anything."

I helped him sit up. He rubbed his elbow and grunted, then I helped him to his feet.

Back in camp, Cassidy told Dad he could go in his kayak and that he'd paddle for both of them. I started to protest, but Dad said, "Thanks, Cassidy. Good idea."

Yeah, thanks, Cassidy, I said to myself. He was doing Dad a favor, but wasn't that my job?

Luckily, Lisa cheered me up. She begged to paddle with me—claiming we'd be lighter than Roger and her, and that we'd fly through the water.

"Okay, Lisa," said Roger. "You'll fly like a dolphin. I'll join Willie in his kayak."

We all helped gather wood for a small, smokeless fire. Ate a light breakfast and tanked up on more coffee. Then broke camp and loaded the rest of our gear on our kayaks, like zombies on fast forward—or at least caffeinated to the gills.

I claimed the rear cockpit before Lisa could—so I could steer—and once Lisa was settled up front, I pushed our kayak into the sea suds, waiting for a backwash to help us out, then jumped into my cockpit.

I felt a little like a sea captain. Nothing could harm us now.

Right?

Only the sound of the sea and the gulls in response.

It's hard to talk when you're paddling a two person kayak at sea, but every once in a while, Lisa paused and half turned and said something.

"So, Aaron, we heard the loon last night—the 'rain bird'—but it hasn't rained. There's hardly a cloud. I guess I got my story wrong."

"Could rain yet!" I said, and splashed her with my paddle.

"Oh my God! I can't believe you just did that! You twerp!" She laughed. "I'm gonna kill you for that!" And she splashed me back. And she got me, good.

"Stop!" I said. "We're falling behind! We have to keep paddling. Seriously, turn around. Paddle!"

"Who made you the captain, anyway! Hah!" She splashed me once more, then turned around and we started paddling, hard.

* * *

All the long day we hugged the shorelines of small island after small island, paddling swiftly, perfectly in sync. It was exhausting but somehow exhilarating, and at this rate, I told myself, we'd make it to the ferry on time the next day.

Tomorrow! I thought.

All of a sudden, I realized that I wanted this trip—which was filled with fear and dread, and a kind of twisted jealousy—to never end.

Life, like dreams, sure can be weird, I thought.

All the good seafood, the wild feeling of adventure, the awesomeness of everything out here—and Lisa, sometimes playful, sometimes sweet—all worked to balance the awfulness of being hunted.

At least, that's how it felt at that moment.

We were flying across the sea, in the lee of a small island, when the light in the sky changed. Dark clouds had begun to gather. Uh-oh, I thought. Lisa's rain bird was right! It felt like a storm was coming.

So when we heard the sound of the *Sea Wolf*, it hit us like a thunderclap.

"In here!" Roger called, pointing his paddle. We followed Roger and Willie through a narrow opening into a large lagoon, encircled by the heavily wooded island. It was slack tide, and the lagoon was as flat as a lake.

It was almost twilight and dark was growing fast. We looked for a place to put in and camp, but stunted spruce grew in a solid mass right down to the waterline. No space for a tent. And we were afraid of being trapped in here if the *Sea Wolf* found us. There was only one way out.

After a quick circuit, we decided to risk being seen by the *Sea Wolf,* and slip back out of the lagoon and seek a better haven.

But when we got to the opening, a tidal rip slashed across the way. The tide was rushing back into the lagoon, like rapids through a narrow gorge.

We climbed out onto some rocks to check it out, then Lisa slid into the rear cockpit before I could get there. "Nice," I said, shaking my head.

Roger and Willie went first and shot through it like pros. Next, Cassidy paddled like the maniac he was—with Dad in front, holding his elbow—and broke through, raising his paddle high over his head, yipping like a coyote.

Now it was our turn. My mouth went dry, my palms were sweating. Here we go! I thought. Lisa aimed our kayak and we paddled like crazy.

But just when we thought we'd broken through, the rip turned the nose of our kayak and hit us broadside . . .

. . . and over we went—*ZWOOP!*

The next thing we knew, we were hanging upside down from our cockpits, clutched by the icy grip of the current— like the talons of an eagle—pummeled by bubbles.

And we couldn't roll back up.

CHAPTER FIFTEEN

THE BARREL OF A GUN

No air. The shock of cold, and our heads down where fishes live. Our whole lives all of a sudden topsy-turvy.

I'd never been taught how to do a tandem kayak roll— and in a fully-loaded two-person kayak, you'd have to be an expert. Instinctively, Lisa and I pushed out of our cockpits and swirled around in the onrush of burning, churning seawater. My life jacket was snagged on something. I didn't know which way was up, and my lungs were on fire. I thrashed and kicked and twisted.

Then, with a bolt of adrenalin, I tore myself free, and shot to the surface.

AIR! Blessed air filled my lungs.

But where was Lisa?

With our kayak bottom up, I thought maybe she was on the opposite side of the hull. All was confusion, with shouts ringing out and a paddle blade poking me in the chest. "Grab it, Aaron! Grab it!" someone hollered. I grabbed it, but then let go. I had to find Lisa first. Where was she?

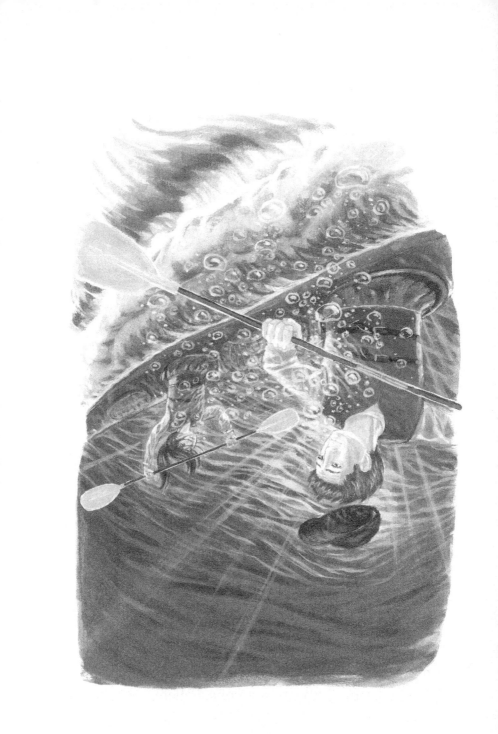

Something banged against the hull of the kayak. I ducked my head into the black freezing water, but saw nothing. I tried to dive down but couldn't get very far—not with a life jacket on.

And just before I ran out of breath and kicked for the surface—*there she was!* Her head bumped into my hip beneath the hull, the tips of her hair swirling up into my face.

I reached down, grabbed her by her life jacket, and kicked for the surface. We both burst through at the same time, gasping for air.

Hooking her life jacket with my left hand, I grasped an outstretched paddle with my other hand. Willie hauled me up by the back of my life jacket till I lay sprawled across the rear hatch of his kayak. Cassidy, with one arm, did the same with Lisa.

Determined to save our kayak before it filled with water and sank, Dad managed to snare the bowline and hand it to Willie, who hauled the sinking boat toward shore.

Roger climbed out of his kayak, splashed through the shallows, and took the rope from Willie. He held our kayak in tow till the rest of us clambered ashore. Then Willie and Cassidy lifted one end of our boat, which allowed some of the water to pour out. Finally they dragged it up on the rocks, still upside down.

Then they lifted the kayak—it must've weighed a ton!— rocked it back and forth, and sloshed out the remaining water.

Lisa and I leaned into each other on a slick rock, our feet still dangling in water.

"Smooth move, dude." Cassidy grinned. He just couldn't help it. He'd pulled Lisa out of the water, after I pulled her up to the surface—but he just had to dis me. By now his attitude should just roll off me like water off a duck.

But it didn't. I tried to ignore him.

"Geez! It was crazy cold down there," I said to Lisa. Dumb thing to say. Her teeth chattered in response, her eyes wide and bloodshot. But by the way she was looking at me, I knew she was trying to say something.

But she couldn't.

We were soaked to the bone, shivering like reeds in the wind. Everything in our kayak had been submerged. We could only hope that the storage hatches hadn't leaked, and that our dry bags had kept our clothes and sleeping bags dry.

The dark clouds, bunched like purple grapes, blotted the moon and the stars. And sure enough, to add insult to injury, the wind started flinging great handfuls of cold rain at us. *Take this! Take that!*

I was going to say something like "You were right, Lisa. The rain bird rules!" But I didn't have the energy and the wind was roaring.

Then behind the roar of the wind, we could hear another sound. Was it distant thunder? Or the rumble of a motor?

Or both?

"If we stay here any longer, with them freezing wet, they

could die of exposure," Willie said. "And the *Sea Wolf* could show up at any time."

"Through my binos, I saw what might be a good place for camping on Hunter Island when we were looking for Lisa," Roger said. "It's not too far from here."

"Good!" Willie said. "We have to find a campsite and build a fire. *Pronto!*"

Lightning ripped the clouds, and a moment later thunder boomed across the sky.

Rain crashed down, then stopped.

That's when we heard it: the unmistakable sound of the *Sea Wolf,* somewhere off in the dark.

"We've got to skedaddle," Dad said.

"You got that right," said Willie. "Let's get this show on the road!"

Dad said he could paddle now though I could see, by the way he cupped his elbow that he was still in pain. There was no time for Lisa and me to change into dry clothes—assuming we had any dry clothes to change into—so all together we flipped my and dad's kayak upright, then we all slogged back into our kayaks sopping wet. Me back with Dad, Lisa with Roger.

And then we pushed off and paddled into the darkness, rounded a point, and wrestled through hordes of whitecaps.

Still weak from exertion and shock, I wasn't much good with my paddle, and my dad—with his hurt elbow—wasn't

much better. Though my body was creating heat with all the effort expended, I couldn't stop shaking. My fingers felt like frozen sausages. I had trouble gripping the paddle, and I was so out of it that sometimes the blade of my paddle missed the water altogether, or just skimmed uselessly across the surface.

Other times I dug too deep and almost flipped us over. But we paddled on—the crippled and the cold. There was nothing else we could do.

Finally, a couple hundred yards off to our right—lit up by a tremendous flash of lightning—was Hunter Island. But as the thunder rolled over us the island sank back into darkness, and we figured we'd have to make a blind landing, where we couldn't see the shore.

Then another bolt of lightning momentarily illuminated a small inlet. We changed course, paddled ferociously, and slid into it on waves of fear.

At that moment, a gunshot blasted a hole in the night.

* * *

If you've never been shot at you can't possibly know what it's like. Nothing prepares you for it. Your body recoils and your heart tries to burst free. You try to disappear into yourself and you forget to breathe and then you breathe too fast and your mouth goes dry and your palms sweat. You want to freeze and flee at the same time. You want to wake up out of this nightmare or fall fast asleep and pretend it's all just a dream.

"WE KNOW YOU'RE OUT THERE!" boomed a voice through a bullhorn.

It wasn't a dream. It was all really happening. We couldn't see the fishing boat in the darkness, but it had to be pretty close.

"WE WON'T HURT YOU. WE JUST WANT TO TALK!"

"It's a bluff," Willie hissed. "They can't see us, and they're not using their spotlight so they can keep us from seeing them. Keep paddling."

So we paddled in frenzied rhythm through the gloom

and into the inlet until Willie nosed his kayak into a slush of gravel-like stones.

"We're in luck," Willie said. "The tide's still far enough out so they won't be able to follow us in."

"Till high tide," Roger said, sliding up beside him. "Or they could drop anchor and come in by dinghy."

"Either way," said Willie, stepping out of his kayak, "we have a window of time and we have to use it. *NOW!*"

In a craze of movement we hauled up our kayaks and buried them beneath fallen branches and kelp. Then we followed our senses—in the brief moments of moonlight between clouds—and stumbled through thick old growth till we found a small clearing.

Exhausted, we dumped our gear and Willie reminded everyone to get busy gathering stuff for the fire.

"Risky, don't you think?" Dad said. "We need heat, yeah, but we don't want to be seen."

"I'll rig up a tarp," said Willie. "So it can't be seen from the water. We're well into the brush here, and it's dark. I think we're good to go. They need a fire and they need it now!"

While the others began gathering wood for a fire, Lisa and I collapsed next to our dry bags.

Our not-so-dry bags.

My teeth chattered, my knees knocked, and Lisa clutched her elbows as if she were trying to fly into herself.

I wished she'd clutch me. I hugged myself and concentrated on not biting my tongue with my clacking teeth.

Again, she turned toward me, as if trying to say something.

But just then Dad brushed the top of my head with his hand. He and Cassidy went back and forth for more fuel, while Willie tried to coax wet wood into flame. Roger said he'd see if Lisa had any dry clothes, but first rigged up a tarp like a lean-to over the sputtering fire, and Willie fed it with the treasure of windfall limbs and sticks.

He was just in time. With a tremendous clap of thunder, a jagged spear of lightning cracked open the night—and again, the rain came driving down like nails.

And this time it didn't stop.

But Willie was a wizard with fire. Though it sizzled and steamed, he managed to keep it roaring while Dad, Roger, and Cassidy pitched tents, and Lisa and I huddled close and tried to warm ourselves and our wet clothes by the flames.

And that's when she said it. "I think you saved my life, Aaron. I came up under the kayak and bumped into it. I couldn't breathe. I kept kicking and kicking. My lungs bursting. And then you snatched me from the darkness."

At first I couldn't speak. I was all clutched up. Then I stuttered, "Yeah, well I, I don't think I would've found you if you hadn't bu-bumped into my hip."

She bumped my hip with hers. I was too out of it to bump her back.

I was trembling so hard my whole body tensed up and felt like one big cramp. A whole-body cramp. My stomach ached with emptiness, and we were in the grips of a chill that shook us in a fist of cold iron. Chill from cold and chill from fear.

Roger called Lisa to come into the tent and change her clothes. She came back a few minutes later in a warm jacket over her dry clothes. She sat back down beside me, leaning into the fire. *"Brrrrrr,"* she said. "I'm still *freeeezing.*"

The rain lashed down and the thunder crashed. The wind moaned like a wounded ghost bear lost between worlds. I put my arms around Lisa, but she just hugged herself, and we shivered together so hard that we both started to laugh—a nervous laugh that wracked us like sobs.

Then Dad came with bad news. Huddling with us beneath the tarp, he told me that seawater had leaked into the hatch and into one of my dry bags when we'd capsized—and my sleeping bag and clothes were soaked.

"Great," I said.

Dad hung my wet clothes and sleeping bag on a line near the fire. He looked at me, like maybe I hadn't secured the hatch well enough. Or closed the dry bag well enough. Or handled the riptide well enough.

He was disappointed in me. He wasn't proud of me. And it hurt.

"Here, dude." It was Cassidy. He offered me a dry flannel shirt and army style camouflage shorts with cargo pockets. Then he held out his sleeping bag. "Just until yours dries," he said.

My mouth dropped open.

"Take 'em, or you'll turn into a frozen turkey!" He pushed the dry clothes into my arms.

"Uh, thanks." I really couldn't believe he'd done that.

I scurried into our tent and changed out of my wet clothes and into Cassidy's. I came back out and everybody laughed—with muffled laughs, like soft coughs. I looked down. The shirt was ginormous, the sleeves down below my hands, and the shorts were almost falling off, hanging down below my knees.

Roger handed me his bandana—he had others—and said, "Here. Better tie those on before they fall to your feet." He almost cracked up, and so did Cassidy.

I rolled up the sleeves and cinched up the waistband of Cassidy's shorts, and tied up the excess with the bandana, kind of like a tourniquet.

Willie handed me a mug. "Here, pard, this'll put a fire in your belly." I sat down and took a sip, then another, and the fiery tea—with maybe some medicinal herb—burned a tunnel to the pit of my belly, and from there it seemed to flow into my bloodstream.

That's when I felt the barrel of a gun rammed up against my spine.

"Freeze!"

CHAPTER SIXTEEN

THE KIDNAPPERS

I froze. Then I dropped my mug.

"Don't move." It was a voice I knew. The captain of the *Sea Wolf.*

What came next happened so fast, it's hard to capture in words. Lisa whipped out her can of pepper spray and sprayed the captain in the eyes. He flew backwards and his rifle went off by my ear with a blast that almost deafened me. The bullet tore a hole through the tarp. Then another man—dressed entirely in black—stepped up to the fire and aimed a speargun right at Willie's gut.

But, unknown to his assailant, Willie had already drawn his hunting knife.

Wild Man Willie let out a hair-raising roar, and flung his knife at the man just as he fired his speargun.

Willie spun away. The spear twanged into a tree trunk—barely missing Willie's belly. Simultaneously, Willie's knife grazed the man's shoulder as Cassidy did a flying tackle around the man's knees. The man dropped his speargun, toppled, and crashed into the fire, scattering sparks like fireflies. Then he rolled out of the flames just as Roger crawled out of his tent. His fishing knife flashed in the firelight.

But at that moment, the captain sat up on the other side of the fire, gripping his rifle and blinking rapidly, tears streaming down his eyes. The barrel of his rifle swung back and forth between Roger, Willie, and Cassidy. Roger held his knife at the ready, while Cassidy, hanging on like a bulldog, kept a lock on the fallen man's legs.

Dad rushed the captain and grappled for the rifle, just as Lisa lunged and bit the captain's arm. I was blown away by her courage! But Dad, still wrestling for the rifle, was no match for the captain, who elbowed him in the face. Inspired by Lisa, I dove at the captain, too, and got punched in the throat.

I gagged at the explosion of pain, clutched my throat, and dropped to the ground like a sack of clams.

Then the captain shook Lisa off, jumped to his feet, and jammed the barrel of his rifle to the back of my head. He glared at Roger and growled, "Drop the knife or he's dead." Roger didn't hesitate. He dropped the knife at his feet. The captain's head twisted toward Lisa. "And you," he hissed, "drop the pepper spray."

Lisa followed his orders, but stared daggers at him.

He rammed the rifle against my head harder and rumbled, "Get up!"

I crawled to my feet and faced him. Strangely, he was wearing his yellow sunglasses in the dark. I saw my doubled reflection in the fire-lit lenses—like a tiny frightened creature trapped inside, surrounded by flames.

I was breathing now, wheezing really, but my throat felt like there was a brick lodged in it. "UP!" he snarled again.

He spun me around and jabbed the barrel of his rifle into my back and started shoving me away from the fire. He kicked Cassidy in the ribs as he walked by. A grunt escaped Cassidy's lips and he finally released the legs of the man in black.

Brushing burning cinders from his sleeve, this guy stumbled to his feet and weaved like a drunkard. His shoulder was bleeding where Willie had nicked it with his knife, but he ignored it. He picked up his fallen speargun, and tried to yank the spear out of the tree trunk, but it wouldn't budge.

"Leave it!" snapped the captain.

The man gave the spear one more jerk, then gave up. Firelight licked his face, and I got a better look at him.

I made out the Chinese geoduck diver, Wong, beneath a black wool cap. With his dark eyes darting in the fire glow, he looked more scared than vicious.

The captain kept jabbing me along. His eyes were scorched red from Lisa's pepper spray, and tears still streaked down his cheeks. "The boy's coming with us. As insurance," he rasped. "You'll find him in Chinatown. Vancouver. Report us, and he'll be a dead duck hanging from a hook in a Chinese butcher shop. Our cargo is money. This boy is worthless."

Still holding the rifle against me, we backed away from the fire circle. Over his shoulder he called out, "And if you try and follow us, you'll never see him alive again."

He turned and we made our way through the woods, followed by Wong.

"Better watch your backs, suckers!" Cassidy hollered.

Knock it off, Cassidy! I wanted to yell. His reckless words pushed me further toward the brink of panic.

* * *

The captain and Wong marched me through the forest and forced me into their dinghy, which was pulled up on the rocks in the inlet. Then they pushed us into the surf and the captain pointed his rifle at me while Wong rowed. My teeth clacked from cold and fear. The rain was just a drizzle now, but the clothes Cassidy had lent me were already soaking wet.

Soon I could make out the dim outline of the *Sea Wolf,* rocking above its anchor chain in deeper water. It looked a lot like the typical commercial fishing boats you'd see in Bodega Bay, but bigger than most. As we drew closer, I thought I could make out the dark shape of the third man from the other night, standing at the helm in the cabin.

The captain forced me up the ladder that hung over the side of the boat, and we boarded the *Sea Wolf.* Wong tied my wrists with rope, and opened a hatch to a hold belowdecks. The stink hit me like a blow to my face—dead fish, gasoline, human waste. Then Wong shoved me down into it.

I landed hard on what felt like slimy dead fish, then crawled over and slumped against the hull, shivering and fighting nausea.

The hatch was still open, so I could just hear the captain talking up on deck. From what I could make out, he was planning to take their boat out of the cove to make Dad and the others think they'd left, so no one would try to follow. "Then we'll anchor around the point in the next cove, out of sight, until first light tomorrow morning. Then off to Vancouver."

With me trapped inside.

Then the hatch slammed shut, locking me in.

A dull orange lightbulb glowed in the hold. I looked around. Dark, haggard Asian faces peered out of the shadows, their bodies draped in ragged scraps.

To my right, an old man said something to me, but I

didn't understand a word. He had white hair that poked out of bony scalp and chin. He was wearing a shiny battered suit that hung from his shoulders like a clothes hanger. Reaching out a shaking finger, he touched the back of my hand, like he was checking to see if I was real.

To my left, a skinny teenaged girl leaned against a middle-aged woman whose mouth opened like an O in a silent wail. The girl was looking at me, her expression hard to make out in the dim light. From what I could see, she was maybe a little older than me. Super skinny, but you could tell she was pretty, with wide cheekbones and deep-set eyes. She was partially bundled in a torn blanket.

Beyond her and the woman, two young men rolled in their blankets, their heads lolling against the hull. And beyond them were three more piles of clothes with people inside them. They were hard to make out. I think they were men, maybe middle-aged. They were lying on the bottom of the hull, atop their blankets. They each had bundles under their heads.

And there were baskets full of stuff and travel bags crammed between them. Tiny living spaces, I guess.

Suddenly I heard the motor start up, and the clang of the anchor chain being hauled in.

My heart went into fast gear. We were motoring out of the cove. Hopefully the next cove was nearby. Hopefully Dad and the others would . . . what? Come and save me?

Hopefully.

We moved slowly. I could feel the swells as we left the cove. I concentrated on trying to slow my breathing down, slow my heart down.

Maybe ten minutes later the motor stopped. We coasted. I heard the anchor being lowered, the splash as it hit the water.

We weren't going anywhere. Not till first thing in the morning, anyway.

I looked around. In front of us, there was a bucket with a ladle sticking out. Drinking water. Beyond that, attached to the far hull, was another bucket. It reeked, even from where I was sitting. I hoped I wouldn't need to use it.

The rain had stopped. The only sound was the creaking of the boat as it rocked back and forth, the slosh of waves against the hull.

"Who are you?" came the soft voice of the girl. She sat up, facing me now. A long braid hung down her back, like a shiny black rope. "Why are you here?" She spoke good English, with a slight accent. A touch of an English accent, actually, above her Chinese accent.

"I'm Aaron. I was on a kayak trip and these guys kidnapped me. They're holding me hostage. Who are you? Why are you here?"

"My name is Shai. We're going to Vancouver," she said in a whisper. "All of us. Some have already paid a lot of money, and we all owe them lots more when we get there, but they treat us poorly. Very little food. Barely enough water. No sunshine or fresh air. Many are sick. Where are we now? How much longer until we reach Vancouver?"

"Maybe two or three more days. But that's just a guess."

Shai said something in Chinese to the others, but no one seemed to be listening. They were all asleep or half asleep. Miserable. Hungry. In pain, by the look of it.

"How long have you been stuck in here?" I asked. My back itched, but I couldn't scratch it. My hands were still tied. They were going numb. My Adam's apple still throbbed from the captain's punch to my throat.

"A very long time," Shai said. "Almost a month. At first they gave us seafood to eat, all thrown together in a pot. Leftovers. But not enough. Never enough. No rice. No vegetables."

I thought about that. A month stuck down in a hold like a cell! Little light. Little food.

"What do you do to fill the time?" I asked.

"It is impossible to fill the time. I have a book to read but it hurts my eyes. Too dark. We talk and tell stories, even try to sing songs, but mostly we just sleep."

The older lady started to sob quietly and to repeat the same words over and over in what I assumed to be Chinese. Shai turned and stroked her bony arms, calming her.

"Now we are scared," Shai whispered. "We don't know what will happen. We are afraid."

I knew how she felt. I was afraid, too.

I tried to loosen my hands. I twisted and yanked and

squirmed, but the rope didn't budge. I felt hopeless, like an otter caught in a steel trap.

Suddenly, panic gripped me like the fangs of a wolf. I stood and yelled at the top of my lungs, "HELP ME! LET ME OUT OF HERE! *PLEASE HELP ME!*"

But who would come to help me? Who would help any of us?

No one.

CHAPTER SEVENTEEN

THE BIG KNIFE

Bile leaped into my throat as the hatch banged open and a black rush of terror poured into me.

The evil captain climbed down the ladder and kicked me in my side with his booted foot, knocking me sprawling. I banged my head on the bottom of the cold dark hold.

The hatch banged shut again. My head rang like a bell.

"It's better," said Shai in a voice that seemed too mature for her age, "if you remain calm. And quiet."

I took a deep breath, not sure how to ask what I wanted to ask. "Is it really worth it? I mean leaving China, going like this to Canada? You could die."

"My mother . . ." she nodded at the woman who was now sleeping, " . . . is not well. My father was a professor, but he died two years ago. Lung cancer from the terrible pollution in the air where we lived. We are very poor now. I had to stop school last year and work in a factory. Very little money. My grandfather . . ." she tilted her head toward the old white-haired man, snoring against a travel bag, ". . . his only wish is to see his brother before he dies. His brother, my great uncle, is younger. He lives in Vancouver. Has his own business. We will live with him. All these others, they hope to get work in restaurants owned by family. It is very poor in China for most people."

She sighed. "Some get very rich, others struggle to survive."

Shai stopped talking and closed her eyes. "We think it is worth it. But we didn't know it would be this bad. And now we don't know if we will really ever get there. But I trust we will. I have to. There is nothing else."

Suddenly it was quiet, but I didn't know what to say. This was a whole world I knew nothing about.

"Where is your family?" she asked. "Where do you live?"

I sat up, rubbing my head. I wasn't sure what to say after hearing Shai's story. My troubles suddenly seemed less important. "We were camping on an island nearby when they took me. I think that's where my family and friends are. But I'm not sure. I heard the captain say we'll leave early in the morning for Vancouver. I'm not sure how they'll find me there."

My mouth was parched, but I wasn't so sure about drinking the water in that bucket.

"I live in California," I finished.

"California," she said, closing her eyes again. She made it sound like some mythical place. "Disneyland. The Golden Gate Bridge. I want to go to California someday."

I looked at her. She had dreams of a future. How could she be so calm? Shai and her family were being treated how I imagined people in the African slave ships had been treated. Maybe not quite that bad, but still pretty awful. I was amazed she could think about anything more than surviving it.

It was a challenge with my hands tied, but I managed to squeeze my right hand into my hip pocket and fish out the Bic pen I always carried for writing in my journal. I found a scrap of paper wedged at the bottom of my pocket, smoothed it out against my thigh, and wrote on it.

"Here," I said, handing it to her. "If you ever get to California—when you get to California—write me at this address. Maybe you could, you know, come and visit sometime."

She took the paper, tucked it into the pocket of her jeans, and gave me a big smile. Then she curled into a ball like a cat, rolled away from me, and nestled her head on her mother's lap. Time to sleep again.

Shai may have been calm enough to sleep, but I was not. What if my dad and the others found us and tried to save me and it all went wrong? Or they don't find us and when we get to Vancouver the captain realizes I'm too big a risk to keep alive? Realizes I could run right to the police if he lets me go.

I might not even make it to Vancouver! He could dump me overboard at any time!

I felt as if my world had been turned on its axis. Suddenly, nausea and dizziness sent me into a panicked daze.

I lay there in my wet clothes, in the dim orange light, and struggled with worry and fear. Fatigue dragged me down like chains. The next day was supposed to be the last day of our kayak trip.

But it could be the last day of my life.

And these people were literally in the same boat. If my dad and the others did try to save me, we might all be held hostage. There could be a violent standoff with no way out but death.

I slid slowly down the hull—as darkness closed over me—thinking, I am going to die.

They are going to hang me up like a dead duck on a hook.

My thoughts went round and round. My mind was a dog chasing its tail.

The dim light got dimmer and dimmer. The ribs of the boat creaked. Finally, I couldn't think anymore and exhaustion swept over me in waves. I drifted away into stormy dreams.

Then suddenly, my mom was shaking me and calling, "Wake up, Aaron. Wake up!"

I woke up, but not to my mom. It was Wong, the Chinese diver, shaking me and hissing, "Wake up! Wake up, boy!"

His eyes looked fierce. His teeth were bared. He pulled something from his belt.

The blade of a huge fishing knife flashed in the dim orange light.

CHAPTER EIGHTEEN

CAPTAIN EVIL

This is it! I thought. Terror gripped my throat like fangs. My dad and the others must've followed us. Now Wong is going to kill me.

"What are you doing?" I whispered. I was crazy scared, but I didn't want to wake anyone else just so Wong could hurt them, too.

Wong held a finger to his lips.

My eyes were clogged with sleep. My body felt like a heap of broken bones. But fear is adrenalin, and my brain was on fire.

He pointed his big knife right at my face.

"You must promise," he whispered, "not to report us. These people paid thirty-seven thousand dollar each to get to Vancouver. Relatives pay same amount when they arrive—if they arrive. They will all get deported if you report us, and I will go to prison."

"So . . . I don't get it." I sat up, still whispering. "Are you letting me . . . *go?*"

"First promise," he whispered fiercely, holding the tip of his knife right in front of my nose.

I nodded. He searched my eyes. The moment stretched on into infinity. The knife trembled in Wong's hand.

I held my breath.

He moved the knife away from my face and quickly sawed through the rope. My hands burst free, along with my breath.

I rubbed my wrists till the circulation came back. Shai rolled toward us, her eyes open, full of shock.

"Why?" I asked Wong. My stomach squirmed like a sack full of eels. This didn't make sense. It was the middle of the night, in the middle of the ocean.

"I'm not a kidnapper, not a killer," Wong said. "I will not go to prison for this. I am a geoduck diver. Legal. I came from Hong Kong two years ago. Now I help Chinese people from Fujian and other provinces come here. But this is a mistake. The captain . . . he is evil. It's all going wrong. I must do the right thing now. Yin yang." He stood up.

Yin yang? "What does that mean, 'yin yang'?"

"Come!" he whispered urgently. "No time now." He started up the ladder to the deck.

It was slowly sinking in. He is letting me go. He is helping me escape! Now it hit me like a surge of electricity.

I shot to my feet and scampered up the ladder. When I reached the open hatch, I looked back down into the hold. Shai stared up at me.

I wished I could take her with me. Take all of them with me. Free them all.

"Come!" whispered Wong, tugging my shirt.

Shai lifted her hand and whispered something I could barely hear: "Maybe I'll see you in California." She was smiling. I started to wave back, but Wong yanked me up on deck and silently lowered the hatch, then jerked his head to follow him.

"What will you tell the captain?" I said as he helped me down the ladder into the dinghy.

"Shhh! I will say you had a knife. Cut the rope yourself. Then cut me." He drew his blade swiftly across the palm of his hand. Blood seeped out, a string of shiny red pearls. I grabbed my own hand, as if he had sliced it instead of his.

"*Now go!*" he hissed. "The next cove." He pointed and scuttled away, silent as a cat.

The dinghy bumped against the hull with each wave. I untethered it and grabbed the oars, climbed in, and started rowing in the direction Wong had pointed.

The *Sea Wolf* seemed to be around a point from our cove. I didn't know how far I had to row, but I did know there would be waves out there. The oarlocks rattled as I pulled with all I had. I put my back into it, used my legs. My brain flashed to the last time I rowed this desperately: it was in Desolation Canyon when Dad was injured. It was life or death, and I had to row us to safety. It felt like life or death again now.

As I approached the point, lights went on in the stern and the bow of the *Sea Wolf.*

Was Captain Evil awake? Did he hear me when I climbed into the dinghy and took off? Was he coming after me?

Tension bound me tighter than any rope.

Moonlight seeped through ragged holes in the clouds. Just ahead of me, I could see huge boulders at the point, waves crashing over them. I gripped the oars even tighter and started to rise and fall with the swells. Waves broke over the front of the boat, spraying my back and head.

As I rounded the point, the dinghy was hit broadside by an enormous wave. The boat started to flip. I slung my weight toward the wave, leaning into it, and my boat slid down, then rose again.

Waves crashed. The surf boomed. I battled with the sea . . .

. . . until finally, finally, I was riding the surf into the next cove. What a rush! I coasted for a moment, then rowed

again. There was no time to lose. I had no idea when and if the *Sea Wolf* would come after me.

At last, deep into the cove, a bird whistle floated my way. *Dad!*

It was like a song from home. I whistled back, softly, and continued rowing toward shore.

Dad and Cassidy splashed out toward me, grabbed the bow, and pulled me in.

"You okay?" Dad almost shouted.

"Yes! I'm alive, right?"

"Hey! I was about to come save you, man!" Cassidy said as he helped me out of the dinghy. His face was blackened with charcoal, like a commando. "I had this whole plan—"

Dad cut him off. "Later, Cassidy, right now there's no time."

I was about to say, "It's a good thing you didn't come. You woulda got me killed!" But in that instant I understood something. Again. Something I'd learned last year in Desolation Canyon.

I realized that yes, Cassidy was macho, irritating, and full of himself, but a part of me envied him. His strength. His courage. And even though his rescue plan probably would've added to the danger, his goal was to cover my back. To save me. Like he'd saved Dad.

Dad drew me into a silent hug. I think he was crying. Lisa ran up and kissed my cheek. I pulled away from Dad, but she'd already stepped back.

"There's no way we were going to leave you," she said.

I looked out into the cove. We were all in danger. Captain Evil would want blood. My blood, especially.

"Shouldn't we hide the dinghy?" I asked.

"Actually," said Roger, "if we leave it here and they see it, they'll come in first to see if we're still here. That could buy us time."

They had already broken camp and loaded the kayaks. They were ready to go. Now we lugged the kayaks one by one to a stretch of shoreline that was around a point in the opposite direction of the *Sea Wolf.* We would be making our run to Bella Bella today, where we would catch the ferry back to Port Hardy.

If we made it without getting caught.

"What happened out there, Aaron?" Lisa asked. She was

right behind me, helping carry a very heavy kayak. "How did you escape?"

"That diver, Wong, cut my rope while the others slept."

"Why would he do that?" she asked.

"He said something about 'yin yang'."

"What does that mean?"

"I have no idea."

As we lowered the last heavy kayak to the small, sharp stones where the water lapped, there was a stillness like before a storm. Our ears were tuned to every sound. If I'd heard a motor just then, I think my heart would've exploded.

On the western horizon, the full moon balanced on the water, like the slightest wave would knock it over the edge of the world.

I felt like that, too.

CHAPTER NINETEEN

GO GO GO GO!

Soon after we launched out to sea and were about to round the point, we heard it.

A motor!

My heart slammed against the inevitable. There was no out-paddling a fishing boat with a large inboard motor. We couldn't possibly escape. But did we stop paddling?

No! We paddled like there was no tomorrow. We swooped through the swells like psychotic swans rearing to take flight.

Willie bellowed, *"Go go go go!"* But we didn't need to be told. Our bodies knew what to do.

This is how survival works. Some kind of ancient memory in our DNA.

The wolves are coming! The wolves are coming!

While I paddled, my ears strained to hear the sound of the motor. Was it getting louder? Was it coming closer?

I couldn't tell. Waves crashed against the cliffs. My heart crashed in my chest. Our paddles slashed the water in a frenzy of motion.

A controlled frenzy. Dad in front, me in back, steering.

We were paddling for our lives!

Just ahead of us, Lisa was paddling like a pro, her hair flying behind her like a banner.

What would they do if they caught up to us? Would Captain Evil try to shoot us, one by one, like ducks in a barrel? Or would he just come after me?

Or Lisa. Take one of us hostage again.

Or try to sink us all?

My mind churned, like our paddles.

Waves boomed. Gulls cried.

Suddenly—I heard the surge of an engine!

And it was getting closer. And closer.

It sounded like it was right behind us!

I turned around. A fishing boat, maybe two hundred yards away, was barreling right toward us, the prow slicing through the water, gushing like twin fountains.

My heart clutched, and my body froze. I couldn't breathe.

But I had to. We all heard it, saw it coming. We all dug in with our paddles and tried to do the impossible: out-paddle the *Sea Wolf!*

What else could we do?

The boat drew closer. There was no time to even look over our shoulders.

This time there was no getting away.

CHAPTER TWENTY

BELLA BELLA

At the last minute, the very last second, the boat veered toward deeper water. We heard laughter as the wash of its passage lapped against our hull and rocked us in the giant cradle of the sea.

It wasn't the *Sea Wolf* at all!

The fishing boat was powering away. And with a flood of relief, we coasted up to Roger and Lisa's kayak.

It was time to regroup. Willie and Cassidy turned back and joined us in a huddle, rolling gently in the swells. Cassidy yipped for joy.

"Jerks," Willie said, glaring at the disappearing fishing boat.

"Well, at least no one got hurt," Roger said. "And it wasn't the smugglers, thank God. But we have to keep going."

I looked back. It still wasn't very light out, but no more boats were coming our way. Now we were out where other boats would be common. Not a place to be shot at by human traffickers.

"I don't see the *Sea Wolf*," I said. "And I don't hear their motor. I don't think they're chasing us. At least right now. I heard the captain say they would leave for Vancouver first thing in the morning. Maybe they're heading full throttle for Vancouver now! Or checking the cove to see if we're gone."

"We should keep moving anyway," Roger said. "They could still be coming for us."

"I don't think they'd risk it out here," I said. "This girl I met down in the hold, Shai, she said they paid—and still owed—big money to be taken to Vancouver. I don't think they'd try anything in the channel with other boats around, and the sun coming up."

Everybody scanned the horizon. A couple of distant islands. A freighter off in the distance—the first we'd seen in days.

"Maybe you're right, mate!" Roger beamed.

Cassidy tried to splash me with his paddle. He missed. Then he grinned and flashed me the Rock On sign.

I could breathe again.

We all could.

"But just in case," Willie said, "we keep moving."

"Bella Bella, here we come!" hollered Roger. He dug his paddle in and took off.

"Bella Bella here we come!" we all yelled, and dug in our paddles as well.

All day we kept on paddling, hard, glancing over our shoulders, listening. Always listening.

Just in case.

And by the time the sun had risen into the low clouds, I could feel the ropes that bound my chest—*SNAP!*

And we were free!

* * *

Soon we were far up Hunter Channel and there were fishing boats and barges and small freighters in every direction. I breathed in the whole sky, and let it out.

Nothing was going to happen to us now.

"Aaron," Dad said out of the blue. He still paddled in front and let me do the steering. "I'm so proud of you, kiddo."

"What?" I couldn't believe I'd heard him right.

"I said that I'm proud of you. The way you escaped from the *Sea Wolf* unharmed. You didn't do anything foolish, something that would've got you hurt, or brought harm to the rest of us. You were very . . . well, mature. And brave."

I stroked through the water, the rhythm as natural to me now as breathing. I'd gotten my "sea legs," as Roger had said I would. I didn't say anything, but I was beaming—as proud as could be. Dad didn't know how much his words meant to me.

But I kept looking back over my shoulder, thinking about the starving Chinese families trapped in the hull of the *Sea Wolf*. Especially Shai.

"Dad? What does 'yin yang' mean?"

"Come again?"

"Wong, the man who helped me escape, when I asked him why, he just said, 'Yin yang.'"

Dad coasted awhile, thinking. The wash of a passing fishing boat lapped against our hull, and another bald eagle soared overhead. "Well, kiddo," he said, "in Chinese philosophy, everything in nature is a combination of yin and yang. An interplay of opposites. Dark and light. Low and high. There's always a spot of one in the other."

Maybe Wong was referring to the spot of good in the evil. He—by freeing me—was the spot of good.

Like a pearl in an oyster, I thought. A rotten oyster.

And I thought about nature. How, in the middle of a storm, there's the promise of calm. And amid the calm, there's the seed of a storm.

"Dad, are we going to report them?" I asked.

Dad started paddling again. "I think we have to, Aaron. As soon as we get to Bella Bella. Those traffickers are dangerous. They threatened you—all of us, really—with death. And the immigrants' lives are at stake. The boat could sink, with all the refugees locked down below drowning."

"But I promised. Wong cut the rope when I promised I wouldn't report them. He cut me free. He even cut himself. He risked his captain's revenge, and he even risked prison. For me."

Dad didn't answer. I kept paddling. The truth was, I didn't know what we should do. Nothing was simple, right or wrong. I felt sorry for Shai's family. They were risking their lives to join their relatives and look for work. Risking tens of thousands of dollars and years of debt. They just wanted to live a good life, like everybody else. But the smugglers, they were doing this for money; they didn't care about freedom or family. They had to be stopped.

But if illegal trafficking was shut down, there would be less chance for other families like Shai's to sneak in. Meanwhile, these immigrants were at the mercy of some very dangerous people.

The more I thought about it the more I realized that I agreed with what Lisa had said: If more immigrants could come in legally, less would fall into the hands of traffickers.

I wrestled with my thoughts, as with a tangle of kelp.

Finally, after ten minutes or an hour—I don't know how long—I came up with an idea.

"Dad?"

"What's up?"

"I was thinking," I said. "We should wait until we're back in Vancouver, and then report the *Sea Wolf*. Shai and her mom and the other families would be with their relatives by then. We could explain that Wong was just a diver, that he wasn't one of them, and that he'd freed me."

Dad was silent a moment. "We'll see, kiddo. We'll see."

That didn't sound like a "yes." I knew what Dad wanted to do, and suddenly I was sure it was the wrong thing.

"Listen, Dad, if the Coast Guard goes after the *Sea Wolf*

before they let their passengers off in Vancouver," I argued, "it would put the families in danger. The boat's not likely to sink now, not after crossing the whole Pacific Ocean. But that captain, he's ruthless. He'd hold them hostage, like he did to me. He'd let them die before he'd give them up. But if we wait until they get to Vancouver, he'll let them go. He wants the other half of his money from their relatives. That's all he cares about: the money. And he'd have no reason to hurt them if he wasn't threatened. He'd sneak into Vancouver and finish his deal, no matter what."

Dad was silent. He was thinking.

And while he thought, the only thing that remained sure and clear in my mind was that we had to do what would give Shai and the other people in that boat the best chance of not getting hurt.

Dad stopped paddling and we coasted. "You're right," he said. "We can't do anything that would endanger the people trapped inside that boat. Good thinking, Aaron."

Wow! I was speechless.

He agreed with me. My dad actually agreed with me!

Something grazed my shoulder. It was Lisa touching me with the tip of her outstretched paddle. I felt as though I'd just been awakened from a deep dream, or risen from the bottom of the sea.

"Hey," she said.

"Hey," I said back, and she smiled.

I floated on that smile—a whole person floating on a

smile—until Cassidy yelled out, "Dude. *Look!*"

Just at that moment, the sun burst through the clouds and poured down an intense light on the old native village of Bella Bella up ahead.

We made it!

We'd come full circle. And one thing was for sure: I felt like a different person from the one who'd started out ten

days before. I felt like a seaman. What Roger called an "old salt."

I looked again at the village in the blazing light, and I thought about the meaning of the name.

"Bella Bella," I said to myself, *"doubly beautiful."*

EPILOGUE

After we drove off the ferry from Vancouver Island, our first stop in the city of Vancouver was at the Royal Mounted Canadian Police station. Roger, Willie, and my dad made a full report. The police told us they would check with harbor officials to see if the *Sea Wolf* had come in. Hopefully, Shai and the others were long gone to safety by then.

I was hoping to see some traditional Mounties on horseback, and there were a few, but most of them were "mounted" in police cruisers instead.

Afterward, we walked through the big city. Soaring over the skyline, well inland from the harbor and the city proper, stood the line of snowcapped mountains we'd glimpsed from our kayaks all along our journey at sea.

Chinatown was bustling, full of great smells, joyful shouts, and some not-so-joyful shouts. We stopped for dinner at a Chinese restaurant. We didn't order geoduck because it wasn't on the menu. Maybe, like Willie said, it was off-season.

I kept hoping I'd see Shai. See her smile. See her safe and happy in her new home. I hoped she had made it. I hoped they all had made it.

And I hoped Captain Evil would get put away where he couldn't hurt anybody ever again.

Dinner was super tasty—and because this would be our farewell party—it was a festive celebration.

When it was time to say our good-byes, I said, "You rock, Lisa!" and gave her a hug. She gave me a funny look, then smiled, and kissed me on the cheek. "You rock, too, Aaron!" It was a little awkward.

Then Cassidy chimed in, "You *rock*, Aaron!" mimicking Lisa.

I laughed and he punched me on the shoulder and said, "You're okay, Aaron. For real. Later, man."

I hoped there would be a "later" next year. We had gone on a wilderness adventure two years running now. I hoped that next year we would go river kayaking through a new wilderness.

* * *

When Dad and I finally got back to Bodega Bay three days later, it was great to be home, to see Mom and my brother, Sean. But the first thing I wanted to do was check the mail. I was hoping for a note from Shai. I knew it was too soon, but I hoped anyway.

I opened the mailbox door, stuck my hand in, and felt around.

A postcard! I yanked it out and looked at it. And when I saw the picture of snowy mountains ringing the Vancouver skyline, my heart soared.

I flipped it over and read:

Dear Aaron,

We are here now in Vancouver, at my great uncle's house! It is all very exciting and a little scary, too. We do not know the future, but we still have hope. I worried you would report us and we would be sent back to China. But I think you did not, and for that I want to thank you.

I hope to see you in California someday.
Your friend,
Shai

I was blown away. I took a picture of the postcard, both sides, and sent it to Lisa and Cassidy.

And the next thing I wanted to do was to put our sea kayak into Bodega Bay.

And so that's what we did. We drove out to the inner bay, just like last time. Another beautiful day. A light breeze, no chop. We carried our kayak down through the rocks and over the sand to the water. The tide was out and we saw white pelicans bobbing in the shallows. Overhead, gulls wheeled and squealed in the bright sun.

Our plan was to paddle out through the channel and into the ocean to look for orcas. Sea wolves. Maybe we'd even hear the call of the loon again.

This time, I didn't capsize the boat when I climbed in.

"See, Dad!" I wanted to say.

But I didn't have to. Dad already knew.

And so did I.

AUTHOR'S NOTE

*B*ella Bella is a work of fiction. But I *did* spend ten days island-hopping in a kayak off British Colombia in 1999, when a large commercial fishing boat was seized off the coast of Vancouver Island. It was carrying over one hundred undocumented Chinese immigrants. The Royal Canadian Mounted Police (RCMP) arrested several members of the crew whom they suspected of smuggling. Authorities discovered that the water used for drinking and cooking the rice for the migrants was contaminated, and that they were sick, hungry, and tired.

And I *did* meet a scuba diver in the sea next to a fishing boat who offered us a huge geoduck clam; he said he was gathering them for his brother who owned a Chinese restaurant in the city of Vancouver. It was illegal to harvest geoducks at that time. I put this together with the news about undocumented Chinese immigrants seized on a fishing boat, and this was the seed of the idea that led to this novel.

Human smuggling and trafficking is big business in Canada. (There's a technical difference between the two: trafficking involves forced labor and threats of violence.) But this isn't limited to Canada. The United Nations (UN) estimates that human smuggling is currently one of the most profitable criminal activities in the world and it's growing at an alarming pace. There are 2.5 million victims of human trafficking around the world, many of them women and children.

There are an increasing number of migrants fleeing political and religious violence in Africa and the Middle East. In April 2015, a boat from Libya capsized on its way across the Mediterranean Sea to Italy, drowning 800 people. In an ongoing humanitarian disaster that began in 2011, millions of Syrians have fled the violent civil war there, with hundreds of thousands of refugees stranded across Europe as they search for new homes.

Refugees from poor countries like Bangladesh and Myanmar (Burma) often pay unbelievably high prices to human smugglers to be transported to wealthier countries in Southeast Asia, like Thailand, Malaysia, and Indonesia, to escape religious persecution and grinding poverty. In May 2015, 350 Myanmar migrants were refused entry into Thailand and were left stranded on a fishing boat by smugglers off the southern coast.

In oceans and on highways around the world, smugglers are abandoning boats and trucks, taking the money but leaving migrants without food or water, sometimes locked inside with no way to escape.

Desperate migrants all over the world take huge risks and pay their life's savings to smugglers for a chance at a better life. These migrants are facing a crackdown by border patrols and sometimes armed vigilante groups. And when caught they are often put into harsh detention camps—children, too—and usually deported.

Almost everywhere, the response has been more focused on protecting borders than on protecting the rights of migrants and refugees. As the director of the human rights group Fortify Rights says, "This is a grave humanitarian crisis demanding an immediate response. Lives are on the line."

There are no easy answers, but answers must be found. Kids can get involved and learn more from organizations such as.

Fortify Rights

International Organization for Migration
    (run through the UN)

Migrants Rights International

Amnesty International

DISCUSSION QUESTIONS

1. In what ways is Bella Bella *a story about overcoming fear?* Give three examples from the text to illustrate this theme.

2. Often, stories tell you a great deal about their characters without stating it directly, leaving it to the reader to **infer** information from surrounding detail. The adventure in this story takes place on a sea-kayaking journey. What can you **infer** about each of the characters based on this choice of vacation activity?

3. How do the characters in this story differ in their views on race? Lisa comments that Cassidy's best friend is nonwhite. Does having a friend of another ethnicity give a person license to be more critical of other cultures? Why or why not?

4. Characters in Bella Bella discuss the use of various terms to describe native cultures and people of other races. How is language and word choice important when discussing culture? Give examples from the story.

5. The characters in this story are faced with the real-world problems of human trafficking and undocumented migrants. What have you heard about this topic outside of this book? How are Aaron's views on the subject affected by what he encounters on his kayaking adventure? How do his views compare with other members of his traveling group?

6. How is Bella Bella similar to another book you've read? Cite examples from both books to support your comparison.

7. How would you describe Aaron's feelings about his father? Does their adventure affect their relationship? How? Did the story leave you with any questions about the two of them?

8. When the adventurers all throw rocks at the bear to scare it away from the island, Aaron picks up a stone but doesn't throw it. Why do you think he chooses not to join the others in throwing rocks at the bear? Give evidence from the text to support your answer.

9. Other than overcoming fear (mentioned above), what is one major theme of this story? What main ideas do you think the author wants you to take away? Support your answers with examples from the book.

10. The author describes various animals as having unusual interactions with the native people who live along the

Northwest Coast. Describe one such animal, including any native name and/or related folklore presented in the book.

11. Describe Aaron's relationship with Lisa. How does the presence of Cassidy affect how Aaron acts toward Lisa? Give examples from the story.

12. How would this story be different if there were no adults involved? In what ways do the adults drive or influence the decision making in the story? In which situations were the adults least involved in the direction of the plot?

13. The diver from the Sea Wolf describes his actions in terms of "yin and yang." What does he mean by this? Can you find other examples of yin and yang in this story?

14. Why does Aaron ask his father to delay alerting the authorities about the smugglers? Do you agree or disagree with his decision? Why?

15. Why do you think the author chose to name a story so full of danger Bella Bella?

Best-selling author **Jonathan London** has written more than one hundred picture books for children, many of them about wildlife. He is also the author of the popular Froggy series. He lives with his wife in northern California. www.jonathan-london.net

Sean London received a BFA from CalArts in Character Animation and has done animation for Disney. He has collaborated with his father on *Desolation Canyon* and the upcoming *Grizzly Peak* and *Pup, the Sea Otter.*

CPSIA information can be obtained at www.ICGtesting.com
Printed in the USA
BVOW06s1233260116

434238BV00004B/4/P

9 780882 409238